C000063284

SENSE & SCENT ABILITY

A NORA BLACK MIDLIFE PSYCHIC MYSTERY
BOOK ONE

RENEE GEORGE

BARKSIDE OF THE MOON PRESS

Sense and Scent Ability

A Nora Black, Midlife Psychic Book 1

Print Edition March 2020

ISBN: 978-1-947177-34-5

ISBN:

Publisher: Barkside of the Moon Press

PRAISE FOR RENEE GEORGE

"Sense and Scent Ability by Renee George is a delightfully funny, smart, full of excitement, up-all-night fantastic read! I couldn't put it down. The latest installment in the Paranormal Women's Fiction movement, knocks it out of the park. Do yourself a favor and grab a copy today!"

— —ROBYN PETERMAN NYT BESTSELLING AUTHOR

"I'm loving the Paranormal Women's Fiction genre! Renee George's humor shines when a woman of a certain age sniffs out the bad guy and saves her bestie. Funny, strong female friendships rule!"

— -- MICHELLE M. PILLOW, NYT & USAT BESTSELLING AUTHOR

"I smell a winner with Renee George's new book, Sense & Scent Ability! The heroine proves that being over fifty doesn't have to stink, even if her psychic visions do."

— -- MANDY M. ROTH, NY TIMES BESTSELLING AUTHOR

"Sense & Scent Ability is everything! Nora Black is sassy, smart, and her smell-o-vision is scent-sational. I can't wait for the next Nora book!

— —MICHELE FREEMAN, *AUTHOR OF HOMETOWN HOMICIDE, A SHERIFF BLUE HAYES MYSTERY*

PARANORMAL MYSTERIES & ROMANCES

BY RENEE GEORGE

Nora Black Midlife Psychic Mysteries

Sense & Scent Ability (Book 1)

For Whom the Smell Tolls (Book 2)

War of the Noses (Book 3)

Aroma With A View (Book 4)

Spice and Prejudice (Book 5)

Age of Inno-Scents (Book 6)

Aroma Holiday (Book 7)

Grimoires of a Middle-aged Witch

Earth Spells Are Easy (Book 1)

Spell On Fire (Book 2)

When the Spells Blows (Book 3)

Spell Over Troubled Water (Book 4)

Ghost in the Spell (Book 5)

Peculiar Mysteries & Romances

You've Got Tail (Book 1)
My Furry Valentine (Book 2)
Thank You For Not Shifting (Book 3)
My Hairy Halloween (Book 4)
In the Midnight Howl (Book 5)
Furred Lines (Book 6)
My Wolfy Wedding (Book 7)
Who Let The Wolves Out? (Book 8)
My Thanksgiving Faux Paw (Book 9)

Witchin' Impossible Paranormal Mysteries

Witchin' Impossible (Book 1)
Rogue Coven (Book 2)
Familiar Protocol (Booke 3)
Mr & Mrs. Shift (Book 4)

Barkside of the Moon Paranormal Mysteries

Pit Perfect Murder (Book 1)
Murder & The Money Pit (Book 2)
The Pit List Murders (Book 3)
Pit & Miss Murder (Book 4)
The Prune Pit Murder (Book 5)
Two Pits and A Little Murder (Book 6)
Pits and Pieces of Murder (Book 7)

Hex Drive

Hex Me, Baby, One More Time (Book 1)
Oops, I Hexed It Again (Book 2)
I Want Your Hex (Book 3)
Hex Me With Your Best Shot (Book 4)

This is for all the women over fifty who still feel twenty-nine in their heads.
You are me, and I am you.

ACKNOWLEDGMENTS

I have to thank sooo many people for this book!

First, Michele Freeman and Robbin Clubb, my critique partners, who tirelessly poured over every chapter as I wrote the book, and gave me so much feedback. This book is amazing because of them!

Second, my favorite Cookie in the whole world, Robyn Peterman, my other critique partner. She is one of my biggest cheerleaders. Her support makes me feel like I can conquer the world!

Third, to my editor Kelli Collins, who is not only a super fabulous grammar queen, she is also my lifeline. She has pulled off magic in the way she turns around these edits.

Fourth, to the readers and my Rebels, without you all, what would be the point? I am so happy and blessed to have you guys in my corner!

Fifth, but not least, coffee. Thank you strong black coffee for once again being there for me through every step of the writing process. You are a wonderful gift to me and humanity.

BLURB

My name is Nora Black, and I'm fifty-one years young. At least that's what I tell myself, when I'm not having hot flashes, my knees don't hurt, and I can find my reading glasses.

I'm also the proud owner of a salon called Scents & Scentsability in the small resort town of Garden Cove, where I make a cozy living selling handmade bath and beauty products. All in all, my life is pretty good.

Except for one little glitch...

Since my recent hysterectomy, where I died on the operating table, I've been experiencing what some might call paranormal activity. No, I don't see dead people, but quite suddenly I'm triggered by scents that, in their wake, leave behind these vividly intense memories. Sometimes they're unfocused and hazy, but there's no doubt, they are very, very real.

Know what else? They're not my memories. It seems I've lost a uterus and gained a psychic gift.

When my best friend's abusive boyfriend ends up dead after a fire, and she becomes the prime suspect, I end up a babysitter to her two teenagers while she's locked up in the clink. Add to that the handsome detective determined to stand in my way, my super sniffer's newly acquired abilities and a rash of memories connected to the real criminal, and I find myself in a race to catch a killer before my best friend is tried for murder.

ONE

"I think I have a brain tumor," I blurted as I flung open my front door for my best friend, Gillian "Gilly" Martin. She held a bottle of wine in one hand and a grocery bag filled with honey buns, potato chips, salted nuts, and chocolate-covered raisins in her other.

"You don't have a brain tumor." Gilly passed off the bag and the bottle, then brushed past me, shrugging off her coat and hanging it on the hall tree. It had been a cold March, with temperatures in the low 40s most days. Under the coat, Gilly wore a form-fitting, long-sleeved, baby blue turtleneck sweater and black palazzo pants that flared out over a pair of black flats. Her straight chestnut-brown hair was in a loose ponytail for our girls' night in.

"Are you pooping okay?" she asked. "The doctor said you weren't supposed to strain. You could pop internal stitches."

"Quit asking me about my bowel habits," I said. "As

of yesterday, I've been cleared to resume normal activity. Like straining when I poop. Besides, I'm worried about my head, not my butt." After all, my mother had died of brain cancer. "I've been..." I trailed off, trying to find the right words. "Seeing things."

Gilly squeezed my shoulder in an effort to comfort me. "You had a hysterectomy, Nora. Didn't the doctor say you might feel strange for a while?"

Um...if strange included dying on the operating table and then discovering strong scent-induced hallucinations, then yeah. I felt strange. I mean if death was gonna bring me a gift, I would've liked something a lot more useful than the ability to smell other people's troubles.

How could I possibly explain my new weird ability to her? Well, obviously, I couldn't. It had been eight weeks since my surgery, and I still hadn't figured out a way to confide in Gilly.

"Nora?"

I sighed. "I need a drink." I lifted up the wine bottle. "Let me pop this sucker." Gilly still looked concerned, but I smiled and nodded toward the living room. "Be right there."

A few minutes later, I handed Gilly her glass of Cabernet Sauvignon and sat down next to her on the couch.

"You know, regular activities include sex," Gilly said with a little too much enthusiasm. She waggled her brows at me.

"Sex hasn't been a regular activity for me in a very

long time." Two years to be exact. I wasn't a prude. It's just that there hadn't been a lot of opportunities. Between caring for my mother during the last stages of her illness and dealing with painful uterine fibroids, dating and sex were the last things I cared about.

"You are way too hot to be celibate."

"Sure." I patted my swelly-belly. "I've gained ten pounds in the last two months."

"You just had your guts cut out," she said with a fair amount of exasperation. Then she flashed me her signature Gilly Martin smile, and added, "Besides, men like women with curves."

I frowned and pinched some of my stomach fat. "It's too squishy to be a curve."

She laughed. "Girl. I got squishy curves all over." She rubbed her tummy. "Including my midsection." She fluffed her ponytail. "And I'm sexy as hell."

I grinned. "You certainly are." I had always lacked the confidence Gilly displayed about her looks and body. She wasn't wrong about her sex appeal. Men were drawn to her like bears to honey.

"Have I told you lately how happy I am that you're back in Garden Cove?"

I rolled my eyes then grinned. "All the time."

"I can't help it. I missed you when you lived in the city." Her sigh held a hint of sadness. "Though, I'm sorry for the reason you had to come home."

Last year, my mother's brain cancer had progressed to its final stage. My father had died ten years ago, and I was an only child. Mom only had me. So, I'd taken a compassionate leave of absence from work as a regional sales manager for a prominent health and beauty line to care for her. It had turned into an early retirement when my employer decided they wanted to keep my temporary replacement, a younger, more cutthroat version of myself. Thankfully, they'd offered me a generous severance package if I would go quietly, including covering medical insurance costs until I qualified for Medicare in fourteen years.

I'd accepted their offer. Spending time with Mom until her final moments had been a blessing. I didn't regret a minute of caring for her. Of course, from the hospice workers, the aides, the nurses, the volunteers who would sit with her while I shopped, and even the chaplain who brought her some spiritual comfort, I hadn't done it alone.

My mother had been the rock of our family, a major source of comfort and stability. When she got sick, she'd minimized the severity of her cancer because she hadn't wanted me to worry. Honestly, I believed she'd beat it. I'd never seen Mom not succeed when she put her mind to something. If only I had known how bad it really was, I would have come home sooner.

Reconnecting with Gilly had been one of the major bright spots since moving back to Garden Cove. We'd been inseparable during elementary and high school. She'd been the maid of honor at my wedding and had done the pub crawl up in the city with me when my divorce had been finalized. I had been twenty-nine at the time. It was hard to believe that twenty-two years had passed since then. When I was in my teens, I couldn't wait for high school to be over so I could make my own life. Then in college, I couldn't wait to graduate so I could be married. Later, when my marriage fell apart, I couldn't wait to be out of it so I could move away from Garden Cove and start my career.

I'd spent so much time wishing my life away that I'd failed to really live in the moment. I didn't want to be that person anymore.

My whole life had been go-go-go, and I was ready for some slow-slow-slow.

I squeezed Gilly's hand. "I missed you, too. You know, it's not too late to quit your job and come work with me in the shop."

Gilly smiled. "I like running the spa at the Rose Palace Resort."

"I know you do." I didn't press her. We'd had this conversation a dozen times since I'd bought Tidwell's Diner and converted it into an apothecary, where I sold homemade beauty and aromatherapy products. I couldn't afford to pay her what she was worth, anyhow. But it didn't stop me from wishing we could spend more time together. I considered myself lucky that she'd had tonight free.

Gilly was a single mom to teenage twins, and the high school was out for their short spring break that would end on Monday and Tuesday thanks to snow days in January that they still had to make up. The kids were doing overnights at their friends, while Gilly had packed a bag to stay in my guest bedroom and leave for work in the morning from here. Hence the wine. "How are the kids doing?"

"Like they would tell me." Gilly snorted. "They're teenagers, so they share as little as possible. Marco seems to be doing okay. He's dating a girl a year older than him. A senior. Can you believe it? I wouldn't have ever dated a younger boy in high school."

"Marco's a good-looking kid."

"He's only sixteen and just like his dad," Gilly agreed. "Oozing charm and confidence. Worries me sometimes."

"He's not anything like Gio," I assured her. Marco, while moody and temperamental at times, had a kind heart, unlike his father, who only cared about himself. The twins never saw their dad anymore, and that was on Giovanni Rossi. After the divorce, he took a head chef position at an Italian restaurant in Vegas. He used his work as a way to avoid parental responsibility. Too often, Gilly carried that burden of guilt, as if it was her fault Gio had abandoned his kids.

"What about Ari?" I asked.

"She made the honor roll." Gilly's daughter's full name was Ariana Luna Isabelle Rossi. A beautiful name, but she preferred Ari. The girl marched to the beat of her own drum, and I loved that about her. Where her mother was hyper-feminine in both hair and clothes, Ari wore her hair like James Dean, and her outfits tended to be androgynous. "She's so smart, but I can't help but worry about her. She's so damned quiet. How in the world did I, a woman who can't shut up, raise a daughter who doesn't like to talk?"

"You got me there," I said, offering a sly smirk.

"Nora!" She smacked my arm. "You're terrible."

"Ouch." I rubbed the spot and laughed. "I really am. Good for Ari, though," I said. "She's always been a smart cookie. And her drive and ambition to excel will take her places." I didn't have children by choice, but that hadn't stopped me from agreeing to be Marco and Ari's godmother. When I lived in the city, I'd sent the kids packages every year for birthdays and Christmas, but I hadn't spent a lot of time with them until I returned to Garden Cove. "She's going to be just fine, even if she didn't inherit her mother's gift of gab." I slung my arm around Gilly's shoulders and squeezed, careful not to jostle our wine glasses.

I caught the sweet scent of raspberries with notes of citrus and vanilla.

Blurry shapes form...a woman stands in front of a large man who towers over her. Faces are hazy. It appears as if they're both made of colored smoke.

"It's over, Lloyd."

I recognize Gilly's voice.

"Don't be that way, Gilly," *the man cajoles.* "I didn't mean anything by it."

Gilly's voice chokes. "I really like you, but I can't be with someone who would say those things. Especially about my daughter. Ari is a great kid."

She turns away from him and he grabs her arm. Gilly gasps as he yanks her against his body.

7

"*We belong together.*" He manacles both her wrists with his large hands. "*You have to give me another chance.*"

"*Get your hands off me,*" she says, pain evident in her shaking voice.

"*I'll never let you go.*" His menacing tone chills me to the bone. "*Never.*"

"Hello." Gilly snapped her fingers in front of my face. "Earth to Nora."

"What?" I said, blinking at my friend.

Her brow furrowed. "Are you okay?"

"You're going to get grooves between your eyes if you don't stop worrying about me." Although, at this point, I had enough worry for both of us. "How is it going with the new guy you're dating? Lloyd Briscoll, right?"

Gilly went pale and the wine glass in her hand trembled. I took it from her, then placed both of our glasses on the coffee table. "Gilly?"

"I'm fine," she said, her voice pitched to an unbelievably cheery tone. "Didn't you promise me a date with Mr. Darcy?"

I'd wanted to tell her about my scent-stimulated hallucinations, and maybe now was the time. This was the first...er, vision I'd had about my best friend. Still... what if I was wrong? If I really did have a brain tumor, and these experiences were a symptom of being sick, then it would be stupid to worry Gilly. Besides, if she thought I was nuts, she might decide to tie me up, throw me in the car, and take me to the nearest emergency room.

But her avoidance of my question, in addition to the vision, stirred a bad feeling in the pit of my stomach.

"Tell me what's going on," I said softly.

Gilly took a sudden interest in a loose stitch at the bottom of her sweater, tugging on it to avoid my gaze. "We broke up." She paused. "Correction. I broke up with him." Gilly pushed up the cuff of her sleeve and revealed finger-sized bruises on her wrist.

"He did this?" I asked. My stomach clenched. What I'd glimpsed of Gilly and Lloyd's interaction had been real. Holy crap. Without thinking, I asked, "Was it something to do with Ari?"

Gilly gave me a sharp look. "How did you..." She shook her head then nodded. "I overheard him laughing with some of his buddies in the security office." Her hands were shaking now, and there was anger in her voice. "They were talking about Ari." Her eyes narrowed as her ire surfaced. "He called Ari a freak, and some other unsavory slurs that I won't repeat, because she happens to wear her hair short and the way she dresses."

I took her hand and gave it a pat. "He's an asshole."

"I marched right into that room gave him the it's-not-me-it's-definitely-you speech. He grabbed me and told me we were done when he said we were done."

"Is that after he told you he'd never let you go?"

Gilly paled. "Yes. How did you know that?"

Alarm kicked my adrenaline in. I skipped her question and went right to the important part. "That's a threat, Gilly. You need to call the police."

"And tell them what? Who's going to believe Silly Gilly over the head of security for the Rose Palace? Lloyd is an ex-cop, and he still has a lot of friends on the force."

"Yeah? Well, so do I."

"You mean your ex-husband chief of police who you haven't spoken to in ten years? That guy?" Gilly scoffed. "Shawn Rafferty didn't like me when you two were married."

Shawn and I had divorced for a myriad of reasons, but mostly because he'd changed his mind about wanting kids. I had not. When we divorced, we split everything down the middle, and since we didn't have children and we were both just starting our lives, I didn't sue for alimony. I didn't want anything tying us together anymore. Not even a last name, so I took back my maiden name. And then poof, like magic, it had been as if the five years we were married and the four years we dated never existed.

But say what you want about my ex-husband, he's a good cop. And, yeah, a good person. He and his wife had sent a lovely spray of lilies for my mom's funeral, and Shawn had even stopped in at the visitation. Our conversation, the first one we'd had since my dad had died a decade ago, had been short but not unpleasant.

"Shawn will believe you." I clasped both of her hands and looked her in the eye. "Promise me you'll call the police if that son-of-a-bitch comes within fifty feet of you again."

"We both work at the Rose Palace. Our paths are

bound to cross." Gilly blew out a breath. "But I'll do my best to avoid him."

I stared at her hard, my mouth set in a grim line.

She raised her hand as if taking an oath. "And I'll call the police if he attempts to even talk to me." She pushed my shoulder lightly. "Now, come on. I didn't come over here to lament my tragic taste in men. You promised me a night of binge-watching Jane Austen movies, good wine, and all the popcorn I can eat."

My smile felt tight. Gilly was an adult, and she'd been living her life just fine for many years without me telling her what to do. "You're absolutely right. Let's fill up these wine glasses, and I'll start the popcorn. You break out the goodies." Like a weirdo, I loved mixing chocolate-covered raisins in with my salty popcorn. Yum.

Twenty minutes later, we were sitting on my comfy couch with throw blankets over our legs, a large popcorn bowl between us and honey buns on the coffee table. Our wine glasses were full of Cabernet Sauvignon, and our undivided attention was on Mr. Darcy.

"Why can't real men be like him?" Gilly bemoaned after Darcy gave Elizabeth moon eyes.

"No, thank you," I told her. "I like the fantasy of Darcy, but he's judgy and bossy and arrogant. Give me a guy who is genuinely interested in my happiness, and not what he *thinks* will make me happy. That's the guy I'll spend the rest of my life with." Not that I thought such a man existed. I wasn't content exactly, but I was resigned to living out my life as a single woman. I glanced at Gilly. At least, I knew I'd never be alone. Not with friends like her in my life. I nudged her and smiled. "Even so, I'll happily root for Elizabeth Bennet to get her man."

"So, you are looking for a man," Gilly said triumphantly.

"You're the worst," I said.

Gilly made a kissy face in my direction. "Best Bitches Forever."

High-beam headlights glared through my living room window. I shielded my eyes and waited for them to go off. They didn't.

"Who is that?" Gilly asked. "Were you expecting anyone?"

"No. Just you." I got up and looked outside with Gilly right behind me.

"Oh. Oh, no," she hissed. "It's Lloyd."

"Go lock the front door," I said. When she didn't move, I said with more force, "Now!"

Gilly took off toward the front door, and I moved quickly up the stairs to my bedroom, ignoring my creaky knees as I retrieved my gun case from my bedside table. My hands were trembling as I opened the case and grabbed my compact 9mm and a full clip of bullets. I loaded the gun while I returned to the front of the house.

It was dark outside. "Is he still out there?" I asked.

"Gilly!" I heard a man shout. "Gilly, come talk to me. I just want to talk. I'm sorry about earlier. I didn't mean it. I swear. I promise it won't happen again."

Gilly had her body pressed against the wall and out of sight. "I think he turned off the light so he could see inside," she said. "He won't stop calling for me."

"How did he know you were here?" An awful thought occurred to me. "The kids?"

"No," she said. "They're staying the night with friends." She shook her head. "I told him a couple of days ago that I was coming over here to celebrate your recovery." Her pitch went up a notch as tears flooded her eyes. "I'm so stupid."

"He's stupid. Not you."

"Gilly!" he bellowed. "Come out and talk to me. Don't make me come in there after you."

"That is just about enough." I loaded a round into the chamber of my pistol and stalked to the door. "Call the police," I said.

"I already did," she said. "What are you going to do?"

"I'm going to get that jerk off my property."

I unlocked and opened the front door, walking out with my weapon extended in front of me. The wind whipped my hair across my face, and I pushed it back with my free hand. I hadn't bothered to put on shoes, and the rough concrete from my walk bit into my socked feet. I ignored the discomfort as I took aim at the drunk in my driveway.

Lloyd, a tall man, handsome, even with a receding hairline, gave me a look of sheer incredulity. He wore a dark nylon jacket with a tear in the pocket, his cheek was red and swollen, and his lip was bleeding. I guessed this wasn't the first fight he'd started tonight.

"Get back in your car and leave, Lloyd. And stay away from Gilly," I said. "The police are on their way, and if you're gone before they get here, I won't file a complaint."

"You can't shoot me." He laughed. "Castle law means I have to be in the place you live. Otherwise, you'll go to jail for assault or attempted murder."

"The way I see it, I can shoot you, then Gilly and I can drag you into the house."

He walked up to me and pressed his chest against the barrel of my gun. "Go ahead, tough girl. Shoot me."

The sour scent of beer mixed with whiskey made my stomach roil.

I recognize his out-of-focus form before the reek of booze confirms it. "Bitch!" Lloyd yells. He grabs a red-haired woman, his hands encircling her throat. Like Lloyd, I can't make out her face, and with her knees buckled, I can't tell how tall or short she might be, but I can feel her desperation. She struggles to escape but he is too strong.

"Please," she whispers, barely audible. "You're...choking...me."

He throws her to the ground and straddles her, his thick hands squeezing her throat. But who's his victim? I'm helpless. She's dying. He's killing her.

I snapped out of it, full of rage. I lifted the 9mm higher and aimed at Lloyd's head. Something in my eyes must have frightened him because he took several steps back.

Sirens sang out in the distance.

"Tick-tock," I said to Lloyd. "A smart man would already be in his car."

He scowled at me. "Crazy bitch." On that note, he jumped into his vehicle, started it up, and squealed his tires as he reversed out of the driveway.

Gilly came running outside clasping a butcher knife. "Oh my gosh, Nora. You're a freaking superhero."

"When the police arrive, I'm filing a report," I said, trying not to pass out.

She whipped the knife around in the air. "But you told Lloyd—"

"Gilly, stop waving that thing before you hurt yourself."

She blushed as she dropped her arm to her side. "I forgot I was holding it. What are we going to say to the police?"

"The truth. Lloyd Briscoll is a bad guy, Gilly. Like, really bad." I shivered as pieces of the vision played in my head. "He needs to be reported. And you need to show them your bruises. I have a feeling this man isn't going to leave you alone without encouragement."

TWO

The stringent scent of tea tree oil combined with the smoother notes of jasmine was a welcome relief as I stirred the essential and perfumed oils into a large pan of melted glycerin. I inhaled deeply, trying to calm my nerves.

Last night's scratch-and-sniff vision featuring Lloyd the douchebag had really freaked me out. I'd wanted to tell the patrol officers about it, but what could I have said without sounding certifiably insane? Oh, and by the way, Lloyd might have strangled a woman sometime in the past. What does she look like? Red hair. Face, blurry. Eyes, blurry. Any distinguishable marks? You mean other than blurry?

Yeah. Sure. I could totally see my accusation getting the serious attention it deserved. And honestly, I wasn't sure if what I'd *seen* was real or an overactive imagination.

I waved my hand over the pot, inhaling the calming

scents again. Right now, I just wanted to surround myself with delightful smells that wouldn't instigate murderous memories.

Pippa Davenport, my one employee, poked her head into the workshop. "Nora? Why are you hiding out in the kitchen?"

"It's not the kitchen, Pips." I waved my hand around. "No food is prepared here."

Pippa was a thirty-something blonde, willowy, and fine-boned. She was one of the most loyal people I've ever had the privilege of working with. I'd hired her as my personal assistant when I had been the regional sales manager for one of the top beauty suppliers in the country.

After my mom died, I'd used some of my savings to buy Tidwell's Diner and turned it into Scents & Scentsability, a shop that specialized in homemade luxury bath and body soaps, lotions, and oils. When I was nearly ready to open for business, Pippa had been my first call. She didn't hesitate to quit her city job to move down to Garden Cove, which made her just the right amount of nuts in my book. We'd been running the shop together for the past eight months, with her taking on the lion's share of the work for the last eight weeks while I recovered.

Pippa smirked. "Fine. It's not a kitchen. But if I were you, I'd turn off the stove. You heard about the Still River Steakhouse out on 40 Highway, right?"

"No." Still River was one of the few fine dining restaurants we had in the area. They specialized in aged premium steaks and fresh seafood—well, as fresh as seafood could be in the Midwest. Dad used to love going there, but since my return to Garden Cove, I'd avoided the place. Too many good memories knotted my chest with breath-stalling grief, and we'd had wonderful times at Still River. "What happened?"

"It burned to the ground last night. I was getting coffee at Moo-La-Lattes this morning, and I overheard Fletcher Davis telling Greg Spiers that the fire investigator thinks it was an oven fire that got out of hand." She eyeballed my stove.

"That's terrible." I didn't intend to avoid Still River forever, but now, the choice to go there was gone. It felt like another loss on top of all the others.

One of my dad's pals, Lester Blankenship, used to own the restaurant, but he would be in his late seventies now. I wondered if he was still the proprietor or if he'd sold it to someone else. Either way, having your place of business burn down had to be traumatizing. "I hope the owner had enough fire insurance. Was anyone hurt?"

Pippa shrugged. "Not that I heard."

"You're getting to be a real townie, Pips. Pretty soon, you'll be president of the gossip phone tree," I teased.

She clucked her tongue. "And you'll be the town hermit, growing moldy and hunchbacked as you stir your witch's brew."

"Am I a witch or a humpback hermit in this scenario?"

"I think you can pull both off if you try really hard." She stopped smiling, then gave me a once-over. "You look pale, Nora. Are you sure you don't need more time off?"

"Nope. The doctor gave me the thumbs-up to return to normal activity." I hadn't told her about my run-in with Lloyd. She would worry about me even more and would want to get involved with the situation. Despite being younger, Pippa often acted like my second mother. I'd seen her make CEOs cower. The woman was fierce. "Pippa, there's no need to treat me like an invalid."

"I'm treating you like someone who had major surgery two months ago."

"I'm A-okay," I said. My phone beeped a notification.

It was my biweekly reminder to change my hormone replacement patch. No wonder I was feeling a little run down. I always felt more fatigued the third day after putting a new patch on.

"What's that?" Pip asked.

"Just one of the perks of getting rid of your lady parts. Hormone replacement patches." Pippa was staring at me, and I finally said, "What?"

"The bus dropped off a load of tourists at Dolly's Dollhouse Emporium. They'll be at our place shortly. Since you promised Gilly we would pass out samples, I need you to get your *A-okay* butt out of the *kitchen* and behind the sample counter."

See? Fierce. "I'll be out there in a sec," I said with resignation. It was the resorts' off-season, so the managers had organized tours every weekend in March to generate extra revenue for the town. Gilly, who was on the tourism board, had made sure my shop was approved as one of the stops. I'd been excited at the prospect of getting on Garden Cove's tourism map because, well, cheap marketing. I hated to admit I was shaken up after last night, and I wasn't looking forward to dealing with the retail end of my business today.

"Come on, Nora. What is going on?" Pippa asked as she put her hands on her hips. She squinted at me. "You're not yourself. Are you pooping okay?"

"Seriously? I don't know why you and Gilly are obsessed with my bowel movements." I put up my hand to stop her from talking. "Do not say a word about straining, unless it's related to making soap."

She grinned and held up her hands in surrender as the dulcimer tones of our door chimes shifted her attention.

"Saved by the bell," I said. "We better get out there."

Pippa wagged her bone-thin finger at me. "We're not done with this conversation."

"Hello," a woman called. I recognized Gilly's voice.

I pushed past Pippa, apologizing as I made a beeline to my best friend. "What are you doing here?" I asked.

Gilly's brown eyes lit up when she saw me. "I volunteered to play tour guide today." Her voice grew quiet. "Besides, Lloyd was in his office today, and this was the easiest way to avoid another confrontation." She wore a white puffy winter coat, black wool pants, and gray and white fuzzy boots. "Though, if I'd known how cold it was going to be, I might have given it a pass."

It was thirty-eight degrees out, but most of the snow

from the previous week had melted, so at least people weren't slogging through ice and mud.

"Good. That man is a menace." The farther away she stayed from Lloyd, the better. "Besides, this weather suits you. You look like a gorgeous ski-bunny." I peered out the window at the faces staring from the bus. "How many do we have coming?"

"Thirty-seven on this trip."

"Is that good?"

"They paid four hundred and forty-nine dollars and ninety-nine cents each for this weekend event." She grinned. "So, yes, really good."

"Then you're buying dinner tonight," Pippa said to her.

"I'll tell you what," I countered. "As a big thanks to both of you, Pip, for holding down the fort while I was out, and Gils, for bringing in business, I'll take you both to the Pit for dinner." The Bar-B-Q Pit had the best ribs in town. Always falling-off-the-bone tender and seasoned with the tastiest dry rub southeast of Kansas City, Missouri.

"Oh." Gilly rubbed her hands together. "I hope they have burnt ends tonight."

"And don't forget drinks," Pippa added. "Of the alcoholic variety, of course."

"I can't guarantee the burnt ends." I laughed. "But drinks are a given."

Gilly looked out the storefront window. "They're coming. You ready?"

"Send in the clowns," Pippa said dramatically.

I raised my brow at her. "Those clowns will keep us employed."

"Have I told you how much I love clowns?" asked Pippa with a cheeky smile.

"I hope you sell a gazillion soaps and lotions today," Gilly said. She gave me a quick hug as the tourists began to wander in. "I guess I better get to Moo-La's and give Jordy a heads up."

Jordy Hines was the owner of the coffee shop. He had tattoos and was built like a boxer. Pippa liked to make up jobs that Jordy did before he'd landed on barista.

My favorite was handsome undercover DEA agent gets tatted up, infiltrates biker gang, gets injured during the big takedown bust, receives a settlement with early retirement, and uses the money to buy Moo-La-Lattes. If I didn't desperately need Pippa, I'd encourage her to write romance novels. She had a flare for fictional heroes.

I scooted behind the sample counter to man my station. It was filled with tiny soaps and little plastic bottles of lotion I normally sold for two dollars each. I wasn't about to put up samples of my massage oils. For one, I didn't have bottles small enough to make it cost effective. And two, they could get a good feel for all our scents with what I had on display.

There was a sign at the front of my counter that read: *2 Samples Only Per Customer*

"Oh, I definitely want the magnolia blossom and the pear and basil," said a woman with black hair, tasteful makeup, and wearing a pink fur-lined coat.

"No problem," I told her. "Do you want those in soap or lotion?"

"Can I have each in both?" she asked.

Inwardly, I groaned. She was neatly put together with simple jewelry, suggesting someone who was frugal, meaning, she was the type of person who wouldn't buy the cow if I was giving the milk away for free. I know the metaphor was usually reserved for sex and marriage, but I always thought it fit retail really well.

I put on my most charming smile. "I'm so sorry. I'd love to give you the lotion and soaps in both scents, but I've only enough samples for two per customer. But you are going to love them. I would suggest the magnolia blossom in lotion and the pear basil in the soap. It's really refreshing."

Her mouth turned down at the corners. "Okay. I guess I'll take those."

"By the way," I said. "You have really lovely skin."

That turned her frown upside down. "Thank you." She automatically touched her face and leaned back to look in the mirror behind me. "I'm thirty-nine."

Middle-aged women tended to give their age when complimented. I wasn't judging her, because I did the same thing when people commented about my appearance. "What do you use?"

She leaned in conspiratorially. "I hate to admit it, but I use an ungodly expensive moisturizer I bought when I was on a cruise two months ago."

I was aware of the beauty scheme tourist traps. If

she'd bought into their scam, then maybe she would spend some money for the right product. "Pippa, why don't you show Miss..."

"Darla," the woman supplied.

I smiled again. "Take Darla over to our facial line and let her sample the rose hip and blue tansy face oil." It was mixed with other great oils and really worked. "I use it faithfully day and night," I told her.

"You have great skin, too," she said.

"And I'm fifty-one," I told her in a hushed voice.

She raised her brows then looked at Pippa. "Take me to your face oils."

A man stepped up to the counter next. He had on a pair of dark blue trousers with a gray button-down shirt under a black blazer. Pretty formal for morning attire. "What would you like to try?" I asked.

The corner of his mouth tugged up into a half smile. "I'm not here for the samples, Ms. Black."

His voice was honey smooth, and the way he spoke was almost lyrical. "Are you with the tour?"

He reached into his pocket and pulled out a bi-fold wallet and flipped it open. "I'm Detective Ezra Holden, Garden Cove Police Department."

I wrinkled my nose and spoke quietly when I asked, "Is this about last night?"

"In a way. Can I talk to you alone?" Detective Holden had the brightest green eyes I'd ever seen on a man. He looked to be at least six feet tall, and he wore his sandy brown hair short on the sides and a little longer on top.

He had a few creases around the eyes, but not enough wrinkles to put him past his early thirties.

Suddenly parched, I cleared my throat. "I gave the patrol officers my statement. I don't know if I can add any more insight into Lloyd Briscoll. I made my complaint and that's that."

"I'm not here about the domestic disturbance call."

"It wasn't a domestic disturbance. He stalked my friend to my house then threatened to come in after her."

"Then you threatened *him*," Holden said. His expression and tone never changed. Still honey smooth. "With a gun."

"I have a right to protect myself and my property. I know the law, Detective Holden." I held his gaze, but foreboding sat heavy in my stomach. "If Lloyd is trying to press charges—"

"He is," he interrupted. "He filed a restraining order this morning against you."

"This is ridiculous. I filed a complaint on him. He's the bad guy in this situation, not me." If he intended to shock me, mission accomplished. "Follow me." I whistled at Pippa. "You have the store front," I told her. I led Detective Holden back to the workshop. With a gesture, I indicated he should sit on one of the barstools at the metal table where I cut my soap and mixed my massage oils and lotions. Instead, he leaned against the edge of the table, so I did the same. I'd been raised by a cop and then I married one. I knew their tactics fairly well. If he stood and I sat, he would be in a literal position of power —towering over me. No, thanks.

"In what twilight zone world did a judge grant that idiot a restraining order?" I asked.

Holden crossed his arms over his chest. "You pulled a gun on the man."

"I was in fear for my life," I said. I wasn't going to admit in any way, shape, or form that I was at fault. Lloyd Briscoll was the asshole. Not me. "I'm allowed to protect myself."

"Did he threaten you?"

"He stalked my best friend to my house," I said. "He was drunk as a skunk and threatening to break into my home."

"You could've stayed inside. Waited for the police."

"You're right. I should've waited for him to knock down my door and try to hurt us before I took action." I crossed my arms. "Lloyd physically assaulted my best friend. She broke up with him, and he *stalked her to my home*. That's unstable behavior in my book."

"Mine, too," said Detective Holden. He cleared his throat. "Did your friend file charges against Lloyd for the assault?"

I waved my hand around the workshop. "Does this look like a lawyer's office to you? I don't speak for her, Detective."

The cop's full lips twitched as though he was trying to prevent a grin. He managed to keep his gaze steady on mine, his expression serious. "Is your friend okay?"

"Gilly's got a few bruises, but other than that, she's

fine." I picked up my ladle then slammed it down on the counter. "I can't believe that jackass filed a freaking restraining order against us."

"Not us, just you." He opened his jacket and pulled a sheaf of papers out of an interior pocket. He handed the bundle to me, his gaze conveying regret. "I'm sorry, Ms. Black. I believe you." He blew out a breath. "I'm serving you with an ex parte order of protection. You must keep one hundred feet away from Mr. Briscoll. The full protection order hearing is scheduled for Wednesday. It's likely that once the judge hears your side, the order will be dismissed."

"That bastard." I shook my head. "How did he make this happen so quickly?"

Holden didn't answer, but I could tell by his expression he was asking himself the same question. Gilly had said that Lloyd used to be a cop and that he was still connected. Had he pulled some strings?

"Did you work with Lloyd before he left the department?" I asked. I twisted the papers in my hands. I wanted to tear them all into little pieces and throw it like confetti over Lloyd's head. But I probably couldn't do that from a hundred feet away.

Holden gave me a considered look, then said, "I'm with special investigations, have been since I was hired. Briscoll was a patrol officer. And from what I know, he left about six months after I arrived." He paused for a moment, sniffed the air, then gazed at me with those green, green eyes. "Is that jasmine?"

"Yes. I was making soap earlier. Are you a fan?"

"It was my mother's favorite scent when I was growing up." He leaned over the counter and inhaled. "That takes me back."

Unfortunately, it took me back as well.

"Ezra," a woman says. She wore an unsightly purple sweater with a penguin stitched into the front and blue pants, maybe jeans. "Look how beautiful the flowers are," she said. "Don't they smell delicious." Her face was blurry, as she grabbed a squirming, small, green-eyed boy and hugged him to her. "Where are you going? Don't you try to get away from me." He threw his arms around her neck, and she said, "Now give me a good smack." She patted her cheek.

The boy giggled and kissed her.

"You're such a good boy, my easy-peasy."

"Easy-peasy," I murmured when the memory vanished.

"What did you say?" Holden asked. His surprise quickly turned to concern. "Are you okay? The blood just drained from your face."

"I'm fine." I waved him off. "You were saying?"

He chewed his lower lip for a moment as if considering whether or not to say more. More apparently won. "Keep your distance from Briscoll. Don't even aim a dirty look at the man, okay?"

"Do you know something I should be aware of, Detective?"

"Nothing I'm at liberty to talk about." He straightened his jacket. "One hundred feet, Ms. Black. No closer."

"No problem. It's not like I want to be around the man."

"You can file an ex parte against him," he said. "So can your friend."

"Well, that sounds like a circle of hell. Look, I don't want trouble. So as long as Lloyd stays off my front yard, I'll stay away from him. I don't even need this." I lifted the paperwork and shook it. "I'll happily avoid that jerk."

He nodded. "See that you do."

The warning in his voice was enough to make the hairs on the back of my neck stand up. Detective Holden nodded goodbye then left the workshop. I leaned against the counter, frowning.

What was the detective not telling me?

THREE

Rustic wooden booths with cushioned bench seats were set up in five sections inside the spacious Bar-B-Q Pit. Two sections front and back on either side, and one long section down the middle. The smell of smoke and spices permeated every inch of the place. The owners, Rita and Nancy Little, had mounted a giant metal pig statue behind the hostess counter that had been there for thirty-nine of the forty years the restaurant had been in business. According to legend, they'd won it in a ribs challenge against the owner of a barbeque chain in Kansas City. I ordered ribs to go at least once every two weeks, so I believed it.

"How many for dinner?" the hostess, a woman named Didi, asked. She couldn't have been more than twenty. She was cute with short, spiky platinum-blonde hair and several face piercings.

I saw Gilly and Pippa in a booth by a window toward

the back. I waved as they lifted their drinks in my direction. "I'm with Margaritaville back there," I said.

"Oh, them." Didi grinned. "Go on back. Your server will be over in a minute." It appeared my friends had started the party without me.

My knees, my back, and my feet ached from the long day of standing. The doctor told me I would be more easily fatigued for a while, but I literally felt as if I'd hit a wall. If I hadn't promised my friends dinner and drinks, I wouldn't have come. As it was, I had vegged on the couch until the last possible minute. I hadn't even bothered to shower because I didn't have the energy to restyle my hair or redo my makeup.

"Nora!" Gilly stood up and hugged me. "You're late."

"And you're tipsy." I smiled and took my phone out of my purse. "Besides, I'm on time. We said seven. It's seven. I'm exactly on time."

"What happened to the woman who told me five minutes early is ten minutes late?" Pippa inquired as she scooted over to make room for me on the bench.

"Haven't you heard? That woman died." I put my cellphone on the table and set my purse down. "Get it? Because I flatlined on the operating table."

"That's so morbid," Pippa said with a laugh. "I like the way this night is starting."

Gilly rolled her eyes. "You survived. That's what matters."

"That's me. Well, me and Gloria Gaynor. We survive." I suddenly felt flush, and my back was damp with sweat. "Christ, it's warm in here." Near the center of the table was a faux hurricane lamp with the lit candle in it. I pushed it away from me toward the window.

"I'm a little chilly," Pippa said, rubbing her arms.

"You're red as a beet, Nora." Gilly touched my forehead with the back of her hand. Such a mom move. "But you don't feel feverish."

My phone beeped again. *Change HRT* came up on the notification screen. "Crap. I'm having a freaking hot flash." Detective Holden's visit had rattled me, and I'd completely forgotten about putting on a new hormone patch.

Which reminded me, I still hadn't told Gilly about Lloyd's restraining order.

"That would be a great name for a drink," Pippa said. "Hot flash. Cinnamon schnapps, Fireball whiskey, and Tabasco."

"Gross," I said.

"Sounds like a hot flash for your butt," Gilly said.

"Double gross." I giggled. "But funny."

"Darn tootin'." Gilly snickered.

"No one light a match," Pippa joked.

"I think I'm way too sober for this conversation."

"Oh, Nora," Gilly said. "We've only had one drink."

"Too many," I added.

A young man wearing tight jeans and a tight black t-shirt with a giant pig design across the chest laid a menu on the table in front of me. He smiled and ran the fingers of his right hand through his short dark hair. "Hi, I'm Todd. I'm your server. Is it ladies' night?"

"Something like that," I said.

He gave me a chin nod. "Do you know what you want to drink?"

I wanted to order something strong, but I had a sinking suspicion I was going to be the designated driver. "I'll just take a Diet Coke."

"Nooooo," Gilly said. "You have to have something stronger than that."

"I was having pain earlier," I lied. "So, I took some medicine."

"Diet Coke it is," Pippa said.

Todd winked at Pip. "I'll give you all a few minutes to look over the menu."

"Did that toddler just wink at you, Pippa?" Gilly teased.

Pippa, who was normally pale, turned a bright shade of pink.

"Leave her alone, Gils."

Todd came back to the table. He set the soda down. "Need more time?"

"I don't," I said. I'd been thinking about the ribs all afternoon. "This is all on one check. I'm going with the half slab of baby back ribs, the maple pecan sweet potato mash, and fried okra."

Pippa tapped the menu. "I'll have the same, only sub steamed broccoli for the fried okra. Lots of extra butter."

"And I'll take the burnt ends." Gilly crossed her fingers. "You still have some left, don't you?" The burnt ends were popular, but not infinite, and they tended to go quick.

Todd gave her a crooked smile. "You're in luck. We have a couple servings left."

"Yes." Gilly gave a little fist pump in celebration. "I'll take coleslaw and baked beans as my sides."

"I'll get those orders right in," Todd said. "Can I get any more drinks?"

"I'll take another Hurricane Punch," Gilly said. "Since Nora's driving."

"In that case," Pippa agreed, "I'll have another Blue Lantern."

"And put those on my tab as well," I told him. After all, Gilly might take the news about Lloyd's restraining order better if she was liquored up a little first.

"So," Pippa said. "Gilly told me you went Dirty Harry on her ex-asshole last night. How come you didn't tell me? I mean, I spent the whole damn day with you."

"It was Gilly's business to share. Not mine."

Pippa's eyes widened. "Is that why that hot detective came to the shop this morning?"

"He wasn't that hot." I kept my eyes on my phone, mostly to avoid Gilly's gaze. I could feel it settling on me like warm hands.

"Nora, you're sweating," Pippa said.

I grabbed a paper napkin and patted my forehead. Freaking useless patch! The first two days were great. The third day wasn't usually too bad either, except for the insomnia, but I was pushing four days on this one, and it was pushing back. "I'm fine."

"Tell me about this detective," Gilly said.

Pippa raised her brow and grimaced. "Was it a secret?"

I rolled my eyes. "Not anymore it isn't."

"Give." Gilly curled her fingers at me. "And don't spare the hotness."

"It wasn't a date." Although, if it had been a date, it wouldn't have been the worst I'd ever been on. That was reserved for Carter Price, who thought it would be fun to take me to a free food demonstration at a camping expo. I'd gotten rid of Carter but kept the cookware. "Gosh, this place smells good."

I only hoped the strong aroma didn't trigger any more delusions. I hadn't quite figured out when or how they happened, and while some of the things I saw felt like pleasant memories, others, like Lloyd strangling a woman, were horrific. I scanned the room and saw a couple of tables with people I recognized. "There's the Brashears," I said, waving back at Reba when she met my gaze. She was the real estate broker who'd sold me my house, and her husband, Hal, was a loan officer at the bank. They were a match made in fiscal heaven.

"You're changing the subject," Gilly said as she looked over at them. She smiled. "Oh, hey. There's my neighbor, Mr. Garner." At a booth across from the Brashears, an elderly gentleman with a full head of gray and silver hair, thin, but not frail-looking, sat alone drinking a beer and eating a fried pork tenderloin sandwich. "Aww. I'm glad he's getting out. He hardly ever leaves his house this time of year."

"Why?" Pippa asked.

"His wife passed away in March several years ago, so he sort of becomes a shut-in right around now. I sometimes drop food by. Martha Edison, the homeowner's association secretary, arranges a schedule with some of us."

"That's really nice of her," I said.

Gilly smirked. "I think she has her sights set on him. After all, he's not bad looking for his age and still has his hair and his teeth."

Pippa laughed.

"One of these days someone is going to be saying the same thing about us."

"Land sakes, I hope so." Gilly laughed then her expression sobered. "So, what did Hot Cop want?"

"His name is Detective Holden," I corrected. "And it's not what you think."

Gilly narrowed her eyes at me. "Just spit it out. I know it's something bad or you would have already left me three voicemails and ten text messages about it."

"Lloyd filed for a restraining order this morning."

She sat upright and pressed her hand to her chest. "Against me?"

I shook my head. "Nope. Just me. Apparently, I'm not allowed to be within a hundred feet of him."

"This is a load of horse crap," Gilly said. She was digging around in her purse.

"What are you doing?"

"I'm calling Lloyd to tell him what a piece of—"

"Don't," I said. "It'll just make things worse. I'll get a chance to tell the judge my side of the story on

Wednesday. Until then, we should both keep our distance."

"Are you talking about Lloyd Briscoll?" Pippa asked. She turned to Gilly. "Please don't tell me you dated him."

"'Fraid so." Gilly sighed.

"What do you know about him?" I asked Pippa.

She got very excited. "I heard that Briscoll was forced out of the police department."

"Where in the world did you hear that?" I asked. Then shook my head. "The coffee shop."

"I can't help it if Moo-La-Lattes is small, but the lines are long. People are going to talk, Nora. It's human nature. And I'm a good listener," she explained.

"That's one word for it," I agreed.

Gilly didn't laugh. It seemed the conversation had completely sobered her. She tapped the table. "What did you hear?"

"I heard some woman he'd pulled over had filed a complaint against him, and that the department had settled it with her quietly, but part of the deal was Lloyd had to go."

"How have I never heard this?" Gilly asked. "Cripes, how can I be such a terrible judge of men?"

"Especially when you're such a good judge of friends." I reached across the table and took her hand. "Some men are really good at showing you exactly what they want you to see. That's their fault, not yours."

"If you had a penis, I'd marry you," she said.

"If I had a penis, I'd be gay," I told her.

She did laugh this time, hard enough to make her

eyes water. She dabbed at them with her napkin. "God, I love you, Nora."

I gave her a fond smile. "I love you right back."

"Hey, what about me?" Pippa asked.

"We love you," Gilly said gregariously.

I nudged Pippa's shoulder with mine. "Of course, we do."

A ruckus at the hostess stand drew our attention. Gilly's mouth dropped open. Pippa and I turned to see Lloyd Briscoll.

"I want to talk to Ricky, right now!" Lloyd demanded.

Didi, the hostess, looked visibly upset. "I told you, he's not working tonight."

"Don't you lie to me," Lloyd said. He shook his finger in her face. "If he doesn't come out and face me, I will march into the kitchen and drag his ass out here."

"I'm telling you, he isn't—"

"Ricky!" Lloyd shouted. He slurred the name a little, and it appeared he'd been drinking.

"I've had enough," Gilly said. She stood up from the bench.

"Gilly, no," I whispered harshly. But I was too late, she was already storming off in his direction.

"Crap, crap," I muttered, scooting out after her. I could see this ending badly in so many ways.

"Get on out of here, Lloyd," she said. "You're scaring this girl, and she hasn't done a damn thing to you." Gilly's face was filled with fury.

He blinked, looking almost confused, as he stepped back while Gilly laid into him.

Then he saw me, and his confusion cleared. "You." He pulled his phone from his jacket. "I'm going to have your butt tossed in jail for violating the restraining order."

"I was here first," I protested.

"You think that matters?" he seethed. "You are a dangerous bitch, and I'm going to make sure everyone in town knows. No one will care that your daddy used to be sheriff by the time I'm done with you. I'll ruin you."

And then Gilly lost her mind. "You look at Nora, go near Nora, talk about Nora, or threaten her again in any way, and I will end you, Lloyd! Do you hear me? I will end you permanently!"

Oh boy. There were some things that if you say them in public, you can never take back. Unfortunately, threatening to kill someone is at the top of the list.

CHAPTER

FOUR

"Whoa there, mister," said a young man as he and two of his friends grabbed Lloyd and held him back. I'd seen them sitting at the bar just a few feet away, and I was grateful they'd decided to help.

Two uniformed officers arrived and took over trying to restrain Lloyd and avoid his wild punches. Didi, Gilly, and I moved several feet away as the officers intervened.

"Stand down, Briscoll," one of them said.

"I have a restraining order," he argued.

"You're the only one who needs restraining!" Gilly shouted.

Oh, Lord, how much was bail? Because the way my BFF was going, we would need it before the night was over.

Another officer, a female by the name of McKay, ushered our group away. We returned to our table. I noted Pippa's pale face and WTF expression. Gilly picked up her Hurricane Punch and took a hard pull on the straw. Lloyd's reaction to seeing me, the police car lights dancing through the windows, and the general chaos in the Bar-B-Q Pit made my head swim. I sat on the edge of the bench seat and put my head down.

"Are you all right?" Pippa asked.

"I'm a little dizzy is all," I told her. "I'll be fine in a minute."

"Someone get Nora some water!" I heard Gilly say. "Do you need to go to the hospital?"

"No." I was embarrassed that I was struggling to pick my head up. "I've just done too much today. Dr. Schnell said this might happen sometimes for a few more months."

"Are you Ms. Nora Black?" the policewoman asked.

I turned my head sideways to meet her gaze. "Yes, ma'am."

"I'm going to need you to come with me."

"This is flippin' ridiculous!" Gilly glared at the cop. "Lloyd is the one who should be arrested. He's the one who started all the trouble."

I didn't correct Gilly, but really, until she went at him, he hadn't even realized we were at the restaurant. Still, I agreed that he should be arrested. The man was a grade-A menace.

Officer McKay frowned, her eyes sympathetic. "I'm not arresting Ms. Black. Just escorting her off the premises."

"It seems to me, Mr. Briscoll violated his own order of protection against me by showing up here," I said.

McKay nodded. "True, but the law is on his side as the victim."

Lloyd Briscoll was not a victim. He was a clear and present threat. I scoffed at the suggestion. "That's rich."

"Even so, that puts you in violation for not leaving as soon as he arrived."

I was too tired to fight Lloyd and his ridiculous restraining order. Truth was, it was a good excuse to go home. "Well, crap." I struggled to stand then grabbed my phone and threw it into my purse, finishing with a heavy sigh.

"Are you okay?" Officer McKay asked.

"She just had surgery," Pippa said. "She's still recovering."

"Is this true?" She raised a brow at me.

I nodded. "But I'm okay to drive home."

"You're not going anywhere, Nora," Gilly snapped. "You shouldn't have to leave because that son-of-peter showed up."

"You have kids to think of, Gilly. Don't get into trouble on my account." I forced a smile. "I'll be just fine."

"Thank you, Ms. Black." The lines between Officer McKay's pretty brown eyes relaxed. "If it's any consolation, I agree with your friend." She cast a scathing glare at Lloyd.

"We'll follow you home," Pippa said.

"I'll be fine." I stood up and leaned against her. "Eat first, then take Gilly home, okay? Use the company card."

I walked ahead of McKay as she guided me with her

fingertips at the small of my back. When we passed Lloyd, the other cop, and the men who had intervened, a waiter walked around us with a slice of pie and a scoop of vanilla ice cream. The strong scent of apples and cinnamon was unmistakable.

A small girl with ginger hair dances around, as a woman, her hair darker, more orange in color, peels green apples. "Princess Peanut," the woman says. "Do you want to help?" I wish I could see their faces, but as always, they are a blurry mess.

The little girl bounces with excitement. "Yes, yes, yes," she chants.

"You can add the cinnamon." The woman sets the girl up on the counter and hands her a cinnamon shaker. Then her head tilts in my direction, her body relaxed. She's happy. "How long have you been there?" she asks.

"Ms. Black," Officer McKay said. She gripped my shoulder and gave me a shake. "Carl, get an ambulance."

"I'm okay." I rolled my head to the side, surprised at all the feet surrounding me. Crap. I was on the floor. "How did I end up down here?"

"You passed out," McKay said. "You're lucky I was right behind you, or you could have really hurt yourself."

"So lucky," I muttered. Hundreds of diners trampled all over the floors at the Bar-B-Q Pit on a daily basis, tracking in dirt, gum, and other gross stuff. And now, I was lying in it. Yuck.

"Give her some room," Pippa said to the crowd that gathered around me.

Pain pulsed behind my eyes. "Can someone help me

up?" I'd had half a dozen visions since my surgery, but this had been the first one that ended with me passing out. "I overdid it today."

"An ambulance is on the way," the other officer said.

I eased myself up. "I'm not going to the hospital. I haven't had dinner, yet. My blood sugar is probably a little low."

Officer McKay knelt next to me. "I can't in all good conscience let you drive yourself home."

"Then I'll find someone to drive me home," I told her. It looked like no one was going to help me to my feet, so I braced my hand against the dirty concrete floor and maneuvered over onto my sore knees so that I could push myself up. I'd been experiencing some aches and inflammation in my knees for a few years now, but since my surgery, they had felt even more stiff. I grunted as I forced my knees to carry my weight to a stand, embarrassed by how difficult it was to get up from the ground. "See," I said, dusting my pants and my arm where they'd touched the floor. "I'm perfectly okay."

"Ms. Black," McKay protested, her hand going to my elbow.

I moved out of her grasp. "You can't make me go." I shoved the front door open and pulled my keys from my purse. I didn't want to sound like a petulant child, but this cop needed to stop treating me like an invalid.

I groaned, audibly, when Detective Holden got out of his truck and headed in my direction. I drew my shoulders back and hugged my purse tight to my side. "I'm leaving," I told him. "Lloyd has nothing to fear from little ol' me."

"I'm just here for dinner," he said. He hadn't been surprised to see me, and I got the sense that he was lying for some reason.

"Uh-huh," I said.

"What's going on?" he asked, but his gaze kept traveling to the front door.

"Lloyd Briscoll showed up and made a general ass of himself," I answered. "So, now I'm going home."

"I wasn't asking you," Holden said. He nodded to Officer McKay, who I hadn't realized was still behind me.

"Ms. Black's recollection is pretty spot-on, Easy," she said.

I cracked a smile. Easy-peasy, his mom had called him. Apparently, she hadn't been the only one.

"However," McKay added, "she passed out in the restaurant, and I think she should get checked out by the ambulance before she tries to drive home."

My smile faded. I could hear the sirens now. I grimaced. "For a moment, Officer McKay, I thought we could be friends," I told her.

"Friends don't let friends drive dizzy," she responded.

"Touché."

Detective Holden nodded. "Reese is right. You should get checked out before you go. Better to be safe than sorry."

So, McKay's first name was Reese, and she called

45

Detective Holden 'Easy.' Were they friends? More than friends?

Speaking of friends... "Nora!" Gilly shouted as she and Pippa sprinted out the front door. Well, it was more of a speed walk. "Wait!" She was holding three foil boxes. "I got our orders to go."

Lloyd Briscoll came out the front door next. He scowled in our direction.

"Welp," I said. "One hundred feet or bust." I wiggled my keys. "Come on, Gils. I'll drop you home."

Mr. Easy-Peasy plucked the keys out of my hands. "Either you let the EMTs examine you, or I'll arrest you for violating Mr. Briscoll's restraining order."

My mouth dropped open. "You wouldn't dare!"

"Try me." He folded his fingers around my keys, his green-eyed gaze filled with determination. "So, what's it gonna be, Ms. Black? Ambulance or jail?"

FIVE

My blood pressure had been a little low, but my sugar levels were normal. Detective Holden's threat of jail stopped me from arguing when Bob the paramedic forced me to drink some electrolytes. At least I'd talked them out of the IV they'd wanted to give me.

"Hey, what's happening over there?" I asked Holden, who had perched himself outside the ambulance bay door.

"Lloyd Briscoll is being arrested for disturbing the peace and resisting arrest."

"Nii-iice," I said enthusiastically. "It couldn't have happened to a crappier guy."

I watched as McKay and her partner put Lloyd in the back of their patrol car. They'd been called about him making a ruckus, not for Gilly poking and yelling at him, thank goodness. Or for me "violating" Lloyd's ridiculous restraining order.

"You have a great smile," Detective Holden said.

"Am I smiling?"

"You are, Ms. Black." Holden grinned. Wow. He had great lips. And those green eyes sparkled with humor, making the smile even more devastating to my fluctuating hormones.

In a moment of weakness, I said, "You can call me Nora." My gaze lingered on his face longer than I'd intended. The detective noticed, and his grin got a touch more wicked.

Wait? What? Oh, no. *No.* I was not flirting with a man who had to be twenty years younger than me.

I looked around as if searching for my handbag, and then made a show of picking it up from the floorboard. "I feel much better."

"Get up slowly, Nora," Bob the paramedic said.

"Yep," I told him. Like I had a choice. My knees weren't exactly spry. Thankfully, the dizziness was gone, so I held steady on my feet.

Detective Holden offered me his hand.

Instead, I grabbed the grip bar on the inside of the open back doors. "I can get myself down."

He shook his head but didn't comment when my knee buckled as I stepped down onto the bumper, making me look like a klutz. I managed to right myself with minimal effort and finish my descent to the blacktop.

I saw Gilly and Pippa leaning against my car, both wearing grumpy expressions. I'd had to kick them out of the ambulance because they both were treating me like a demented grandparent.

I turned to Holden. "What will happen to Lloyd?"

Holden's mouth thinned and his shoulders tensed. "He'll land in the drunk tank." He grimaced. "But chances are good he won't be there long."

"That's too bad. Garden Cove would be better off without Lloyd Briscoll."

"Probably not a wise thing to say to a cop," he said, the corner of his mouth tugged into a half smile. "You get home safe, Nora." My name on his lips made my creaky knees weak.

"You enjoy your dinner, Detective Holden," I replied.

"Dinner?"

"Isn't that why you came to the Bar-B-Q Pit?" I asked.

"Oh, yes. Right. Dinner." He jerked his thumb toward his truck. "I'll probably just grab something at home."

"Why would you..." Oh. I got it now. He'd shown up here because of Lloyd. Was he investigating the jerk? And if Holden was investigating the ex-cop, why? I bet there were a lot of ugly answers to that question. "Do you know something about Lloyd that I should know? Is Gilly safe? Am I?"

"One hundred feet, Nora." He flashed his green peepers at me in warning. "That's the safest solution for all of you."

"According to Lloyd, he's the one who should worry about coming within a hundred feet of me," I countered.

"Even so." On that note, Holden sauntered over to a red truck parked toward the entrance to the parking lot.

After he left, I walked the thirty feet over to my car. Pippa scowled at me.

"Stop glaring at me. I'm fine."

"Making Bob throw us out of the ambulance was not cool," Gilly argued. "You passed out. That's a pretty big deal. And we are your family, and family is going to flippin' worry."

"And fuss," added Pippa. She blew out a breath. "So, you're okay?"

"Bob gave me the all-clear? I am good now. Promise." Except for the small matter of some unwanted attraction to the mysterious Detective Holden. "Do either of you need a ride?"

"I'll leave my car here," Gilly said. "I only had the one drink, but better safe than sorry."

"I didn't even drink half of mine, so I can drive," Pippa said.

"You sure?" I asked. "It's no trouble to take you home."

"I'm good." Pippa reached out and squeezed my shoulder. "As a matter of fact, I'm taking Gilly home, too. You need to go get your feet up and rest."

I sighed. "Yes, Mother." Honestly, I was relieved. Gilly lived on the opposite side of town from me, and I wanted my bed an hour ago. "I'll see you both tomorrow."

Gilly handed me the to-go box. "Here are your ribs." She kissed my cheek. "Love you, Nora."

"Love you more."

Overnight, the temperature increased by thirty degrees, making this the first day of spring that felt like actual spring. "How are you feeling today?" Pippa asked as she set up the sample counter.

I bent at the knees to pick up a lotion that had rolled onto the floor. "Great. Even my joints feel better. Man, it's a beautiful day."

"You sure are chipper."

"And why not? The sun is shining, the birds are singing..." *Lloyd got thrown in the pokey.*

Pippa scooted around the counter and booped me on the nose. "Someone finally changed her hormone patch."

"Shut up," I said on a chuckle. She wasn't wrong. "Girl, I got home last night and the back of my shirt was soaked. I never thought I'd regret leather seats."

"So, what's going on with you and that cute detective?"

"Absolutely nothing," I said. I glanced at myself in the mirror behind our facial products display case.

"I heard him compliment your smile last night."

"It didn't mean anything." I glanced at my slightly blurred reflection and let a hint of smile show. I did have a nice smile, damn it. I wore my reading glasses on a chain around my neck, because otherwise I would lose them. So, like an idiot, I decided it would be a good idea to put my glasses on and lean in for a closer look at myself.

Large pores, hooded eyelids, two deep creases between the brows, and what the heck was that tiny line cutting into my top lip. When had that shown up? Thank heavens I'd waxed my lip and chin this week.

"Stop that," Pippa said, pulling me away from the mirror. "Women are built to pick at everything we see as flaws in ourselves. Magnifying the situation doesn't help."

"It doesn't matter." I gave one last glance back at my reflection. "Detective Holden is probably married, anyhow."

"I bet I could find out for you."

"I'm sure you could, Miss Gossip Girl, but just leave it."

We'd opened fifteen minutes earlier, but there hadn't been a single customer in yet. The tour wouldn't begin until ten this morning, so it was probably going to be a slow start to the day. "If you want to go get some coffee or something, you know, from Jordy, I could mind the store."

She flushed.

"I know you. You have your sights set on the biker barista."

"I like looking at him is all. That's not a crime."

"He is fun to look at," I agreed on a laugh.

The front door chimed with our first visitor of the day. My mouth went a little dry as Pippa side whispered, "Speaking of fun to look at."

I gave her leg a quick smack with the back of my hand.

"Detective Holden," Pippa greeted him as she ignored my pained expression. Then she gave me a direct look before adding, "What a nice surprise. Are you here to pick up something for the wife?"

"I'm not married," he said.

"Oh," Pippa said. "A girlfriend, then?"

He shook his head solemnly, and that's when I really looked at him. His shirt was rumpled, not crisp like it had been the day before. Even his trousers were cut with deep creases. And the areas under his eyes were puffy and dark. This was a man who hadn't slept.

"What's going on?" I asked. "Did something happen?" My hand went to my mouth. He had said that Lloyd wouldn't stay in custody long the night before. Had he gotten out and done something to— "Is Gilly okay?"

Holden rubbed his face. "As far as I know. Can we talk in private?"

Okay, so this wasn't about Gilly. At least, not directly, but I didn't feel relieved. The look on the detective's face screamed serious business. "Follow me." I led him back to the workshop.

When the door closed behind us, I turned to him. "We've got to stop meeting like this," I said as a joke.

"I wish it was under better circumstances, Nora." He leaned his hip against a stainless-steel counter near the range top. "I have to ask for your whereabouts last night."

"Uhm, you know where I was. You were there, too."

"I mean after you left the Bar-B-Q Pit."

"I went straight home."

"By yourself."

"Yes. What's this about?" I felt like a suspect, which I didn't like—especially when I had no knowledge of the crime.

"There was a fire last night at the Bar-B-Q Pit. There's a substantial amount of damage."

"Poor Rita and Nancy," I murmured. My heart went out to the Little sisters. They'd put their lives into that restaurant. "They are probably devastated." I pinned my gaze on Detective Holden. "What's going on? Still River burned down and now the Pit? I'm a small-business owner, Detective. Do I need to worry?"

"Yes," he said, "but not for the reasons you think. Did you go anywhere before you went home? Or did you leave home again at any time after you arrived?"

"No and no," I said. "Tell me what this is about—or do I need to call a lawyer?"

His green gaze studied me in a way that made me shiver. "Lloyd Briscoll is dead."

My chin jerked back in recoil. Shock reverberated all the way to my toes. I clutched the counter. "No, he's not. He's in jail." I blinked. "Did he die in jail?"

"I didn't say that. Now, can you detail your movements for me from last night, starting with the Bar-B-Q Pit."

I felt shaken to my core. Last night, I'd blithely suggested Garden Cove would be better off without Lloyd Briscoll. Now, he was dead. "After I was checked out by the EMT, I drove straight home, ate some ribs and sweet potato mash, showered, and went to bed." I wasn't about to tell him about my hormone replacement therapy stuff.

"You didn't watch any television? Something that would offer a timeline."

"Honestly, I was so exhausted, I fell asleep as soon as my head hit the pillow." I'd had very little sleep the night before last, between Lloyd's visit, the police arriving at my house to take my statement, my rampant insomnia, and Colin Firth. "I'd gotten the best night of sleep I'd had in a while. I got up this morning around five, showered again, ate some oatmeal, and took a walk outside for a little exercise and fresh air." I tapped the counter. "How'd he die?"

"We found him at the Bar-B-Q Pit," he said, not answering my question.

"So...Lloyd is the arsonist, and he died during the commission of a crime." The image of flames crawling around Lloyd's charred body made my legs feel squishy. I sat down on a metal stool.

"Are you okay?" Holden put his broad hands on my shoulders to steady me. "You're not going to pass out again, are you?"

"What's the point of keeping how Lloyd died from me? You wouldn't be here asking me questions if he died in an accident." My mouth dropped open. "I'm a person of interest because he had a restraining order against me."

Holden stared at me, then he nodded as if he'd come to a decision. "I don't want to believe you're capable of stabbing someone to death and then setting a building on fire."

"But..."

"I can't let my feelings get in the way of this investigation." He dropped his hands off my shoulders.

I almost blurted *What feelings?* But common sense took hold of me before the words passed through my lips. "So. Lloyd was stabbed? Wouldn't that be hard to tell until the autopsy? I mean if the body was burned..."

"The knife was still in his chest." Holden shook his head. "And I shouldn't even be telling you that much."

"I'm glad you did." I stood up, moved away from him, and started straightening bottles on the shelves. Organizing was my go-to stress move. "That's up close and personal, isn't it?"

"Usually." He cleared his throat. "Do you know if your friend Gillian Martin went back to the Pit last night?"

I glared at him. "Why would she do that?"

"I don't know," Holden said. "Maybe to pick up her car."

I shook my head emphatically. "No way. Gilly wouldn't have gone back in the middle of the night for her vehicle."

"Nora, I saw your friend leave her car in the parking lot last night. This morning it's gone. Unless someone stole it, she most likely retrieved her vehicle sometime during the night."

The hair on the back of my neck stood up. Gilly wasn't involved in whatever happened to Lloyd, and I didn't want to say anything about her that might make the detective think otherwise.

"She wouldn't stab Lloyd," I said. Okay. She'd carried a knife outside to help me confront Lloyd two nights earlier. But I didn't believe she'd actually use it. "Besides, knifing a guy then burning down a restaurant to cover it up seems more like a two-person job, right?"

"You tell me." He gave me a flat stare as if to indicate that I would be the perfect accomplice.

"Are you serious? I could barely hold myself up last night, let alone help a friend get away with murder." I held up my hand. "Not that any of my friends would do such a thing." Even so, if Gilly had killed the guy and called me for backup, I can't say for sure that I wouldn't have brought the shovels and the black trash bags.

"Ms. Martin threatened the man in front of a room full of witnesses. I believe her words were, 'I will end you.'" He shrugged. "Well, his life's been ended." His gaze pinned mine. "And you told me Garden Cove would be better off without Mr. Briscoll."

I pressed my lips together. I'd been married to a cop long enough to know when I was being led down the primrose path. If he had enough evidence that either I or Gilly had killed Lloyd, we'd be having this conversation in an interrogation room at the police station.

I knew Holden needed to do his job, but it still hurt that he believed I was capable of stabbing a guy and committing arson. Well, I wasn't going to let him bat those baby greens at me and turn me into mush. I would do everything possible to protect Gilly and myself.

Better yet, I needed to find out who actually stabbed Lloyd so neither my best friend nor I were arrested for the crime.

I knew Lloyd had hurt at least one other woman. And I had no doubt the man was a serial abuser. Still. How was I supposed to explain that I had seen one of Lloyd's memories of him choking a woman? "If he got physical with Gilly, he got physical with other women. I'm sure there's a long line of females who'd stick a knife in his chest. And he was known for making his share of enemies."

"Uh-huh." Holden sighed again. I swore the purplish circles under his eyes were getting darker. "I need to talk to Pippa Davenport," he said. "Can I use this space?"

"Fine, but if she doesn't want to talk to you, then you need to leave."

He frowned, his tone brimming with irritation. "I could always take her down to the station for the interview."

"You must think I'm really thick. You know my father used to be the chief of police in this town, right? I know for a fact that she doesn't have to go anywhere for any reason with you unless you have legitimate cause. I've answered your questions, and Pippa can decide if she wants to or not."

His brows dipped as he put two and two together. "Chief Connor Black? I've heard some stories about him. There are still a few police on the job who worked with him. What was that, fifteen or so years ago?"

"About that many, yes." I didn't mention that one of

the police still on the job was my ex-husband, the current chief of police, Shawn Rafferty.

I crossed my arms over my chest. "Now if you don't mind, Detective, I have a busy schedule."

"Of course." He held his hand out. "Thank you for your time."

I paused before taking it. His palm was warm, and his grip firm but not in an intimidating way. "Have a pleasant day, Detective Holden," I said in return.

I gave him a wary glance and followed him to the store floor. He made a beeline to Pippa. She shook her head, and then she nodded.

"You don't have to talk to him without a lawyer," I told her.

She blanched. "Why in the world would I need a lawyer?"

I wasn't about to let Holden ambush her the way he'd done me. "Gilly's ex was found dead last night, and the detective wants you to give him an alibi."

Pippa paled even more then lifted her chin, her eyebrows raising with a defiant air. "I don't have anything to hide. None of us do."

When they went back into the workroom and closed the door, I grabbed my phone from my purse. Gilly was number one on my contacts list. I tapped on her number and waited for her to pick up.

"Hey, girl," she said when she answered. "Can I call you back? I'm grabbing some coffee at Moo-La-Lattes before I head to the resort to wrangle the tourists."

"Did you talk to Detective Holden?" I asked her.

"No. Why would I? You're the one with a crush on him." She gasped. "Did he come visit you again? *Girrrl.*"

"I don't have a crush." Why would Detective Holden interview me and Pippa before talking to Gilly?

In a not-so-hot flash, I got it. He was trying to pin her to a location and time. Say, when Lloyd died and the Pit went up in flames. Detective Ezra Holden wanted enough circumstantial evidence to arrest my best friend.

"Stay put, Gilly. I'm coming to you."

CHAPTER
SIX

The scents of coffee, chai, and vanilla hung heavily in the air as I pushed my way into Moo-La-Lattes. The smells were so strong, I braced myself for weird hallucinations, then sighed with relief when I remained delusion-free.

"Over here." Gilly waved at me from a table near the back. She pointed to a cup on the table across from her. "I got you a chai latte."

My standard order. If my stomach wasn't in knots over Lloyd's death and Holden's investigation, I might feel more excited about getting my favorite drink. I took off my jacket and gave Jordy a nod on my way over. Today he wore his long hair pulled back in a Viking-style braid so that the tattoos on the shaved sides of his head were on full display.

He nodded back. "Hey, Nora."

"Hey," I said, then sat down with Gilly and sipped

the sweet, sweet necessity that was a soy chai latte to steady my nerves.

"I can tell you are itching to tell me something," Gilly said. "So just say it."

One of the unfortunate lessons I'd learned as a cop's daughter and wife was that death notifications were best served swiftly. "Lloyd is dead."

I watched the blood drain from Gilly's face, leaving her pale to the point of sallow. She blinked. "Wh-when? Ha-how?"

"Apparently sometime last night. Did you hear about the fire at the Bar-B-Q Pit?"

"Oh my gosh, yes. I feel so sorry for the Little sisters. They don't deserve this kind of bad luck. Especially with all they've been through this past year. What does that have to do with Lloyd? Did he go back there and start trouble? I thought the police arrested him last night?"

These were all great questions to which I had no answers. But Gilly was acting all kinds of innocent, proving my faith in her. She wouldn't kill Lloyd—and she sure as heck wouldn't hurt the Little sisters by destroying their business. "I don't know any of the details, other than he was found in the burned-down restaurant." I swallowed hard, the chai tasting like ashes on my tongue. "But Gilly...he died from being stabbed."

"S-stabbed? I can't believe it." She blinked, and I swear I saw tears in her eyes.

Lloyd did not deserve her grief. "You're not crying for him, are you?"

"No. Not really. It's just a shock is all. We just saw

him last night." She pressed her hand to her chest. "Do they have any suspects?"

"Yes," I told her.

"Who?" she asked.

I gave her a pointed look.

She stared at me, frowning, until realization dawned. "Oh," she said. "Oh no. Not us, surely."

"Detective Holden stopped by the shop to get my alibi. I think he'll track you down after he talks to Pippa."

"He thinks one of us killed Lloyd?"

"Probably not Pippa, though she's certainly solid as an accomplice. But you threatened him hours before his death," I said. "And I pulled a gun on the jerk and he had a restraining order against me."

"This is bad, Nora."

"I can't disagree. But we have one huge thing on our side."

"What's that?"

"We didn't kill him."

She didn't seem comforted. The chai latte churned in my stomach as I studied her expression. I put my hand over hers. "Gilly, did you go back to the restaurant to pick up your car last night?"

She nodded.

"All right." My neck and shoulders tensed. "How did you get back to the restaurant?"

"I called Terry."

Garden Cove had several taxi services for visitors to get back and forth from the different resorts to town and back, but she was talking about the only driver who worked past ten at night during the off season. Terry Pfaff. He charged almost double what he would charge during the day, but since most of his late-night fares tended to be drunks who couldn't drive themselves home, hardly anyone complained.

"I couldn't sleep. The one drink I had wore off, and I didn't want to leave my car in the parking lot all night. But I didn't see Lloyd. And believe me, I would've noticed if the Pit was on fire."

"Please tell me the twins went with you," I said.

"They weren't home. They stayed overnight with friends."

"Great. Neither one of us have alibis."

I heard the whoosh of the door and felt the cold breeze on my back.

"Hello, ladies," I heard Ezra Holden say.

I looked over my shoulder and glared at Holden as he approached our table. "Why are you here? Did you follow me?"

"I'm here for the coffee, Ms. Black. Running into you and your friend is a happy coincidence."

"Happy, my ass," I scoffed.

"Hey, Easy," Jordy said from behind the counter. "You want the usual?"

Holden loomed by our table. "Thanks. But make it unleaded. I drank a pot of coffee this morning."

Unleaded? Unless it was medically necessary, decaf was just sacrilegious, and as tired as Holden looked, he could definitely use more caffeine. I glanced at Gilly and gave her a "be cool" air pat. She countered with a "You be cool. I'm about to throw up" eye widening. I mentally calculated how much money I had in savings, and if it was enough to get new identities and go on the run. Since a lot of my money was tied up in the business, the answer was, probably not.

After he got his cup of fake Joe, Holden walked over to our table and turned his focus to Gilly. "Ms. Martin, where did you go after leaving the Bar-B-Q Pit last night?"

Gilly had started to sweat at her hairline, and the damp wisps around her face clung to her skin. I took her hand. "She went home," I said, regurgitating what she'd already told me. "I'm sure Pippa can attest to the fact that she dropped Gilly at her house."

"And can anyone vouch that you were home?" Holden asked her.

Not with Marco and Ari out at friends. "No one goes home thinking they are going to need an alibi witness, Detective."

"You have children, right?" he asked. "Marco and Ariana. Twins, right?"

Gilly gave me a look of what-the-actual-eff.

"I didn't say anything about the kids," I reassured her while staring daggers at the detective. "And you know I wouldn't call Ari, Ariana. She would flippin' hate it."

Holden thinned his lips. "Actually, Ms. Martin, your police file includes information about your children."

She blinked up at him and swallowed hard. "You have a file on me? Why?"

The Detective ignored her question. "I'd like to ask you to come down to the station, Ms. Martin."

"I don't want to go to the police station," Gilly said.

"And you don't have to," I told her. "He doesn't have probable cause to take you anywhere."

Holden leaned down and said in a quiet voice, "I'm afraid that's not true. We have a witness that puts you in your car at the Bar-B-Q Pit last night shortly before the fire."

Gilly shook her head emphatically. "That's not true." She met my gaze. "I picked up my car, but I drove it straight home."

"And what time was that?" he asked.

"Uhm, around ten-thirty or eleven."

"The fire marshal says that the fire was started around midnight. Our witness says your car was there around that time. Can anyone vouch that you left before then?"

Gilly wrung her hands. I looked at my best friend and briefly wondered if she'd lied about the time when she'd picked up her car. Surely not.

"Don't say another word, Gilly," I said. My heart raced, making my hands shake. I put them on my lap to hide my reaction from the eagle-eyed Detective Holden.

Gilly nodded. Good. My friend might have terrible taste in men, but luckily, she had excellent taste in best friends.

I glared at Holden. "Who is this witness?" I demanded.

"I can't divulge that information, Nora."

"But you're allowed to lie to persons of interest to trick them into making incriminating statements," I countered. "Which is why Gilly isn't going to say another word until she speaks with her lawyer."

"Absolutely," he agreed. "And you're right, using cunning to get to the truth is in the job description, but that's not what I'm doing right now. The witness described the car as a white SUV. License plate DS4 00T."

My heart sank when Gilly started to cry. "I was home before midnight. I swear it," she said. "Maybe someone stole my SUV, took it back to the restaurant, and...and then returned it after...you know."

"Hush, now, Gils." She was upset for good reason, but I knew some cops set their sights on a suspect and got tunnel vision. Instead of investigating all possible angles, they looked only for evidence that pointed at their person of interest. I hoped Detective Holden wasn't that kind of investigator, but I didn't know him from Adam. Hell, he could have killed Lloyd, for all I knew. He'd seemed very interested in Lloyd before the creep's death, and he'd been secretive about his reasons, too.

Holden shook his head. "The thief returned the vehicle to your house? I assume you would have noticed if it had been broken into—and reported your suspicions to the police." His green eyes lit with excitement as he mistakenly closed in on my best friend as Lloyd's killer.

He tapped his middle finger on the table like he was punching a typewriter key. "Well, Ms. Martin?"

"I...I didn't notice anything wrong." She rubbed her arms and gave me a look of pure helplessness. I couldn't help but notice that the rest of the patrons of Moo-La-Lattes had taken a keen interest in our conversation. The tourists were mildly curious, but the few locals I knew were actually leaning in to get an earful.

I stood up. "Detective Holden. Outside. Now." I looked at Gilly's pale, tear-stained face. "Stay here, Gils."

I marched outside and led the detective to the corner of the brick building, away from the picture windows. I pointed at him, stopping short of poking his sternum.

"The witness was either grossly mistaken or malicious. I would bet every cent I own that Gilly is one-hundred-percent innocent. She doesn't even kill spiders for heaven's sake, and you expect me to believe that she stabbed a man, and then hauled his body inside the Pit then set it on fire to cover up the murder?"

"I don't *expect* you to believe me, Nora. It's not my job to convince you of anything, and I never said he was *in* the fire," Holden said.

I frowned. "Didn't you? You said you found his body in the rubble."

"No, I told you he was found on site."

"Where did you find him?"

"I'm afraid we're not releasing that information to the public just yet."

I balled my fists onto my hips. "But you're telling folks that Gilly is a suspect?"

"Person of interest," he corrected. "And I haven't told anyone anything, Nora."

Every time he used my first name, it felt as if he were getting the upper hand with me, so I decided, even without an invitation, fair was fair. "Let me tell you something about small towns, *Ezra*." I crossed my arms. "Everyone in the coffee shop heard what you had to say. By the end of the day, the Garden Cove grapevine will know you were questioning Gilly about Lloyd's murder."

"That's unfortunate," he said. "But Nora...you need to prepare yourself for the possibility that your friend is guilty."

"I'd believe aliens beamed into the Bar-B-Q Pit and killed Lloyd in a freak probing gone wrong before I'd believe Gilly Martin knifed a man in the chest."

"That's, uhm, super graphic." A hint of smile touched his lips but faded almost instantly. "Unfortunately, though, your opinion doesn't count as evidence," he said quietly. "Now, I'm sorry, Nora, but I have a few more questions for Ms. Martin."

"When you have an arrest warrant for her," I snapped. "Until then, you can talk to her lawyer if you have any more questions."

He sighed, his bright eyes leveling on me. "I hope you're right about your friend, Nora. But I go where the investigation leads."

And, unhappily, one particular road led to my best friend.

"You don't have enough to arrest her," I said. "So be on your way, Detective Holden."

He stared at me for a long moment. "I'll see you soon," he said.

After he walked away, I hurried into the coffee shop.

"I don't feel so well," Gilly said. "I'm lightheaded."

I rushed to her side. "Scooch back and put your head between your knees."

She pushed her chair back with her legs, and I rubbed her back as she tucked down.

"It's okay," I said. "We're going to figure this out."

"Cripes, Nora, I feel like I am living in a bad episode of *The Twilight Zone*," Gilly said from between her knees.

I kept rubbing her back. "Are there any bad episodes of *The Twilight Zone*?"

Her chuckle sounded on the verge of a sob. "You know what I mean. How is this even possible? I swear my SUV never left my driveway last night after I got home. And...and Terry can tell them when he dropped me off at the restaurant, right?"

"Yes," I said. "Can your neighbors attest to your SUV being in the driveway all night?"

She slowly sat up and pressed her palm against her forehead. "I don't know. I'm sure the police will ask but it was around eleven by the time I got home, and neither of my neighbors are night owls."

Gilly lived on a cul-de-sac, sandwiched between two houses, both owned by retirees. One of them had been at the Pit the night before. "Well, let's hope Mr. Garner took his dog out to poop sometime around midnight." Mr. Garner had a little pocket beagle named Godiva. I'd never been introduced to the man, but I'd seen him walking the dog from Gilly's window.

Gilly sat up. "Maybe. Godiva is getting old, so Mr. Garner has to take her out more often. Poor bladder control. We should go and ask him."

"That's probably not a good idea. It's better to let the police handle it."

"They are going to arrest me, Nora!"

I grabbed my jacket off the back of my chair and grabbed my chai latte. "The heck they are. Don't you worry. I've got your back. Let's go."

"You'll have to drive. My SUV is at the resort. Oh, the tour!" She flexed her fingers. "Damn it. I have to coordinate the tour, Nora. This venture is bringing in some much-needed revenue for the resort, and I'm pretty sure I won't have a job if I blow it off. Of course, if I'm arrested for killing their head of security, I won't have a job, either."

"When will you be finished?"

"It's an all-day affair. I won't be able to leave until four this afternoon." Tears welled in her eyes. "I can't lose my job. Ari has a science camp coming up, and it's going to cost me two thousand dollars for her to go. I was making a lot of that money with these tours this week."

"I'll give you the money."

"I can't let you do that, Nora."

I gripped her shoulders, even more determined to help. "Fine. You go back to work. I'll go talk to your neighbors."

"I can't ask you to do that. You have your own business to run."

"I can, actually. Besides, you didn't ask, and Pippa will be okay with me taking a few hours off to help you. She doesn't need me as it is. I mean, she's been running the store for the past two months on her own."

"If you're sure..."

"I am," I told her. "Do you have a lawyer?"

Gilly nodded. "I know a guy."

"Okay, now go give the best tour ever but keep your phone on. I'll call you when I have news." I only hoped that the news didn't end with my best friend being charged for a murder she didn't commit.

SEVEN

Pippa agreed to watch the shop while I did a little digging, but not without making a few demands of her own. I wasn't willing to part with the details because I'd dragged her into this situation too much already. Still, I told her we'd talk when I returned. I just didn't commit to what that conversation would be.

Half an hour later, I pulled into Gilly's cul-de-sac and found two police cars parked in front of Gilly's two-car garage. What the actual what? I was too late. Of course, the police were already there.

Ari and Marco stood on the lawn. What a crappy way for them to spend the last day of their spring break. Marco wore his high school green and gold letter jacket, and had his arms crossed over his chest. He stood between Ari and the police like a protective barrier. Ari picked at the back of her short black hair, something she did when she was nervous.

I parked behind a red truck between the first house

and Gilly's, then jumped out of the car and made my way to the forlorn teenagers.

"Aunt Nora!" Ari yelled when she saw me. She wore baggy boyfriend jeans that were rolled up at the hem, a black bomber jacket, and red Doc Martens boots that I had bought her for her sixteenth birthday. She brushed past her brother and met me at the sidewalk. Marco followed her. "They won't let us call Mom," said Ari.

Pissed-off didn't begin to describe how I felt about my godchildren dealing with this nonsense. "They took your phones?"

"Not exactly." Ari grimaced. "Mine's on the charger inside. The cops wouldn't let me take it."

"Mine's completely drained and I haven't had a chance to get it charged," admitted Marco.

"What are they doing here?" I asked. "Did they tell you?"

"They have a search warrant." Marco was taller than his sister by four inches, which put him right at six foot, but his dark brown eyes and black hair were a perfect match to Ari's. They also had similar noses and mouths, which would mark them as siblings, even if they weren't twins. "The cops won't tell us why they're searching the house. Is that even legal?" He scowled at a uniformed policeman standing just outside the arch of their front door.

"They didn't show you the warrant?"

"They did," Marco admitted. "But it doesn't make sense. They're looking for bloody clothing. Why would they look for bloody clothing in our house?"

"They told us to leave," Ari protested, "and told us we couldn't take anything that wasn't already on our person." Her eyes widened. "They even searched us!" she said indignantly. "What is going on, Aunt Nora?"

I tried to give her a reassuring look, but I'm not sure I succeeded. Inside, I was losing my mind. Two days ago, my life felt like it was getting back on track. I'd recovered from surgery, I could work again, and I was at a point where I could think about my mom without crying. Most of the time. Even with the occasional hallucination, I thought I was finally evolving into a new kind of normal. Now, everything was twisted again.

"You guys stay here. I'll find out what's happening." I handed Ari my phone. "Call your mom. She'll want to know what's going on. And I'll be right back."

As I moved closer, I saw Ezra Holden standing just inside Gilly's doorway. I could feel hot rage travel from my toes all the way up to my brain.

"Officer Holden," I said, ice dripping from my words.

"Detective," he corrected.

"*Detective,* I certainly hope you didn't talk to those minor children without a parent or advocate. No one better even mutter a greeting to them without a guardian present." I let out a growl of exasperation. "I can't believe you didn't allow them to call their mother!"

His brow pinched. "What?" He rubbed the bridge of his nose, fatigue apparent.

I guess it was a good thing that his well-being wasn't my concern. Gilly and her children were my priority right now. "Ari's phone is on the charger upstairs, and you wouldn't let her get it."

"First, I just got here right before you did. Second, I'll send an officer up to get her phone."

"Also, the kids were searched. Which officer performed a search on a sixteen-year-old? I'll need his name for Gilly's lawyer."

"Hang on." Holden waved a uniformed officer over. "Grigsby, did someone search the Martin children?"

I recognized Officer Grigsby from the night before. He had been Reese McKay's partner. She'd called him Carl. He shook his head. "No, sir. We haven't searched anyone."

"Marco!" I gestured for him to come to the door.

He jogged over. "Yeah," he said.

"Were you searched?"

"They made us empty our pockets," he said.

"Were you touched in the process?" I asked.

"No," he said. "Just had to take off my jacket and pull the pockets out of my jeans while they checked the pockets of my coat."

"And what about Ari? She said you were searched."

Marco frowned. "*She* tends to exaggerate."

Great. I'd accosted the lead investigator in the case over nothing. "You could have said that when Ari told me you were searched."

Marco grunted noncommittally.

"Fine," I said resignedly. "Go back to Ari." I looked at Holden. "This is really crappy, you know."

He nodded. "I know. And I'm sorry, Nora. But I have to—"

"Follow leads. You've said that. Repeatedly. But as I told you before, you'd be better served looking somewhere else. Gilly had only been dating Lloyd for about a month, and she's the one who broke up with him. Why would she kill him?"

"That's what I'm trying to figure out. Like I said before, I really hope she didn't do it. But I can't give her a pass just because her best friend tells me she's innocent."

I harrumphed. "Fine. I'm going to wait with Ari and Marco until Gilly gets here or until you all leave when you don't find jack."

"All right," Holden said with a smirk. "You do you, Nora."

"Uh-huh," I gave him a one-finger wave as I walked away. I swear I heard him chuckle.

Ari handed me my phone. "Mom is on her way."

"Well, don't you worry," I told the both of them. "I am going to stay until this is over."

Marco's gaze fell on the front door of the house. "I don't understand what's going on."

I sighed. "You know your mom was dating a guy named Lloyd Briscoll, right?"

"I met him once at Mom's work," Ari said. "He seemed okay. A little too chatty, like he was nervous, but still."

Marco's brow furrowed. "I've seen him, but I didn't

really meet him. Why? What about him? Did he do something?"

"You could say that. Last night, he died."

"Wow." Ari blinked. "How?"

"I don't know." It wasn't a total lie. The autopsy wasn't back yet. Mostly, I didn't feel comfortable telling them that Lloyd had been stabbed. So, I went with a less shocking narrative. "The police suspect foul play."

Ari snorted, but more from surprise than amusement. "Is that why they are searching our house for bloody clothes? This is ridiculous. They can't possibly think Mom had anything to do with it."

"We'll get to the bottom of this. Your mom will not go down for murder. I promise." And I didn't care if I had to move heaven and earth, I would make good on it.

Marco paled. "This is nuts."

"I agree," I told them both. "But right now, your mom is the person they are focusing on. Soon, they will move on to other suspects. Don't you worry." A cool breeze chilled my ears. Damn it. The temperature was dropping again. "Why don't we go sit in my car until your mom gets here?"

The twins crawled into the backseat, and I turned on the engine to warm up the heater.

"What did the guy in the door say?" Ari asked.

"That you're a drama queen," Marco responded.

Ari backhanded her brother in the chest. It landed with a significant thud. "Shut up, Marco."

"Hey," I said. "This is stressful enough without you two arguing. Can we be kind to one another, at least, until your mother gets here and takes over?" I loved the twins, but their bickering of late could make a rabbit's ovaries shrivel. "Did your mom tell you what happened with Lloyd last night, or the night before?"

That sobered them. Ari was the first to speak up. "She called and asked if I was okay. She sounded weird, but she didn't say anything about her psycho boyfriend."

"What makes you think he's a psycho?" I asked. "Did your mom call him that?"

Marco glared at Ari, and she shook her head. "No."

"Marco? What about you?"

Marco shrugged as he stared out the window at the police. "Same. Only, she didn't call. She texted."

"Did she ask you to come home?" Gilly had said that the twins had stayed with their friends. But had she given them an option?

Marco shook his head. "I stayed the night at Buck Pollard's. We watched a video of the Northern Heights baseball team. We play them Friday."

"Pollard. That's the coach's son, right?"

"Yep," Marco said on a sigh.

I gave up on the man-child and refocused my attention to the girl. "And what about you, Ari?"

"No." She shoved her hands in her jacket pockets.

I heard a *row-roo-roo* and saw Mr. Garner, Gilly's neighbor, walking up the sidewalk toward his house with Godiva. This was my opportunity to talk to him before the police could and see if he saw anything last

79

night. I turned around and pointed a stern finger at the twins. "You two stay put. I'll be right back."

I got out on the driver's side and hurried around the back to meet Mr. Garner. He had Godiva on the cutest pink leash that matched her collar. The pocket beagle ran and hid behind Mr. Garner's legs. She gave me a warning bark.

"Godiva," he said gently. "Manners."

The pocket beagle—her fur covered in brown, black, and tan patches—wagged her tail, her ears flopping forward. "She's adorable," I said.

"She knows it, too," he agreed with an affable smile. Gilly had told me he was retired Army and had moved to Garden Cove shortly after his wife's death. Apparently, he and his wife had spent summers at Garden Cove for years. It made me wonder if he'd moved here to relive better times. After watching what my mother had gone through when Dad died, I had a lot of sympathy for him. Sadly, his dog seemed to be the only real company he had.

Speaking of the dog, Godiva must have decided I was okay, because she trotted around her master and consented to a quick pet on the head from me. Mr. Garner handed me a small brown squishy treat.

"Give that to her," he said, "and you'll have a friend for life."

The treat smelled like beef bouillon, and when I knelt down, my fingers closed around the cube and...

"Sit, Godiva," Mr. Garner says.

The small dog sits, her ears perked and ready for the next command.

He holds his left hand up. "Roll over." With his right hand, he makes a rightward twirl motion with two fingers.

Godiva rolls over.

"Such a good girl." She gives a happy bark, and he rewards her with a treat.

Mr. Garner studied me, a worried crinkle in his brow. "Are you okay?"

Oh my. Had I just experienced a dog memory? "Yes," I told Mr. Garner. "I space out sometimes." The puppervision was unsettling. "She must really love her treats."

"She sure does. She's highly motivated by yum-yums."

I wanted to see if the dog tricks I'd seen in the vision were real, so I held up my left hand and tested the theory. "Sit, Godiva."

She sat immediately, her tail wagging hard.

"Roll over," I told her next, mimicking Mr. Garner's hand gesture.

To my great pleasure, she rolled over, and then popped back up for her reward.

"What a good girl," I praised her and gave her the morsel.

Mr. Garner's eyes clouded. "How did you know that she knew that trick?"

"Uhm." I was such a dolt. "I'm a big fan of Cesar Millan."

That seemed to appease him for the moment. "Aren't you a friend of Gilly Martin?"

"I am," I said. "We've known each other our whole lives."

"That's really nice," Mr. Garner said looking past me to Gilly's place. He fidgeted with his keys. "What's going on up there? I saw the police driving past the subdivision's dog park, but I had no idea they were coming here."

I shook my head, unwilling to tell him that my best friend was suspected of murder and that the police had enough to convince a judge to issue a search warrant.

"I think I overheard one of the police say something about last night." I segued into the reason I'd come in the first place. I needed to know if he could alibi Gilly's car for around midnight. She said she hadn't left the house after she came home, and I believed her one hundred percent. Unfortunately, belief wasn't going to clear her name. "You didn't see anything, did you? Anyone who shouldn't be around here?"

Mr. Garner's face reddened, and he wiped his forehead with the back of his hand. "I would have called the police right away. Is Gilly okay?"

"She's okay. What about cars? Did you see anyone pull up outside Gilly's place?"

"There was that car that pulled in around ten-thirty last night. I'm pretty sure it was Gilly's, but I went to bed after that."

At least that jived with what she'd told Detective Holden. Although, the car Mr. Garner had seen could have been Terry Pfaff's. "Did Godiva bark at all or have to go out late?"

He stared up the street toward Gilly's house then shook his head. "You know, Godiva did wake me up once, and I saw headlights stream past my bedroom window. I can't be sure of the time though, maybe it was around midnight. I mean, Godiva never woke me up again. That car probably took a wrong turn. Folks do it all the time thinking this is a through-street instead of a cul-de-sac." He glanced past me. "I think one of the officers is coming this way."

I glanced over my shoulder and saw Holden quickly walking toward us. "He'll probably have some questions for you," I said. "I'll just leave you both to it." And on that note, I gave Godiva a quick ear scratch and skirted back around my car. I slipped into the driver's seat and closed the door.

I think I must have been panting, because Marco asked, "Are you all right, Aunt Nora?"

"You look flushed," Ari added.

"I'm fine," I lied. I was worn out, again. Today had been another big walking day for me.

I yelped when a sharp rap on the window startled me. Detective Holden was leaning down to the passenger-side window. He made a down motion with his index finger. I considered giving him a different finger. Again. Instead, I pushed the button to lower the window. "Can I help you, Officer?"

"I am going to have to ask you to meet me down at the station, Nora."

I gave him a flat stare. "And I am going to have to politely decline."

"The request has come in from the chief. He said, and I quote, 'she can come down voluntarily or in handcuffs, I don't care which.'"

"Ass," I hissed. Marco snorted, and Ari chuckled.

"What was that?" Holden asked.

"You can tell Shawn I'll head down there as soon as Gilly gets here."

"Do you know Chief Rafferty?" Holden asked.

I sighed. "Not well," I said because it had been over two decades, and people change. "But I was married to him once."

Holden squinted at me. "Seriously?"

Before I could answer, one of the uniformed police officers yelled, "Detective Holden, we found something."

My heart sank. I knew whatever they found couldn't be the murder weapon that had been in the body. But the fact that they'd found anything at all didn't bode well for my friend.

"I'm sure there's a reasonable explanation," I said.

Holden thrust his arm through the window to the backseat. He was holding a smartphone. "Here," he said to Ari. "I believe this is yours."

"Thanks," Ari said, taking it.

"There's Mom." Marco had turned in the seat and was staring at the car coming up the street.

I met Holden's gaze. "She didn't do it," I said again.

He shook his head. "I'm sorry," he mouthed, then stood up and headed to where Gilly was parking her car.

A sick feeling festered in the pit of my gut. "Stay here," I told the twins. "Just for a few minutes. Okay?"

Before I could get out of my vehicle, Grigsby, the uniformed police officer who'd executed the warrant, put cuffs on Gilly when she stepped out of her car.

"No," I said. "No!" I rushed toward them, my heart beating a thousand times a minute. "What are you doing?"

CHAPTER
EIGHT

I rubbed my swollen ankles one at a time as I waited outside the chief of police's office. They'd built a new police station in Garden Cove about five years back, so I'd never seen the inside of the building before. The GCPD used to feel like family when my dad had been the chief, and now I was the stranger. I couldn't think about myself right now. I had to do everything I could to make things right for Gilly.

I'd taken Ari and Marco, not without a lot of push-back from the twins, to Scents & Scentsability to hang with Pippa. There was nothing either of the teenagers could do to help their mother, and their presence at the cop shop would only add to Gilly's stress.

I still couldn't imagine what kind of evidence the police had found at her house that would merit an arrest. Marco had said the search warrant had specified bloody clothing. Could they have really found something like that in Gilly's place? No. I refused to believe there was a single piece of hard evidence to support murder charges against my best friend.

This was all a horrible mistake, and I planned to get to the bottom of it.

I looked at my phone screen. Twenty minutes had passed since I'd arrived. Twenty GD minutes. Who the hell did Shawn Rafferty think he was to make me wait outside his office like this? Even if we hadn't seen each other in years, he had to know I was out here losing my mind. Considering Gilly's life was at stake, I was in no mood to play games with my ex. While Shawn and I had parted amicably twenty years earlier, I was seconds from kicking his freaking door down and throttling him.

Finally, the door to his office opened. His graying hair was a little thin at either side of his forehead, creating a widow's peak, and he had a bit of a paunch, but hey, so did I.

He met my gaze. His expression was a combination of sober seriousness and sympathy. "Hello, Nora."

"It's about time," I huffed. I stood up, dropped my reading glasses and my phone into my purse, while ignoring the pain in my feet.

"I'm sorry it took so long. I was on a call with the mayor. This is the first murder we've had in town in a decade."

Mayor Callie Cartwright was the first female mayor of Garden Cove, and it was an election year. It didn't take a political genius to figure out that she was worried about what an unsolved murder would do to tourism. Not to mention two of the town's most popular restaurants being lost to fires, possibly arsons. The town might well lose a bunch of revenue, but it was also likely Mayor Cartwright would lose her job. And while tourism did feed my own business, at the moment, I was more concerned with Gilly being falsely accused of killing Lloyd.

"This is a bunch of crap. You and I both know that Gilly Martin is not capable of murder."

"Same old Nora," he said. "Always straight to the point."

His assessment annoyed me. "Did you want to make small talk first?" I gave him a terse frown. "You didn't invite me down here for afternoon tea, Shawn. You ordered me to your office like a common—"

"Witness," he supplied.

"Criminal," I amended.

"Look," Shawn said, stepping back from his open door. "Come on in so we can talk about this."

I jammed my fisted hands down to my side and strode past him into the room.

Dark wood panels balanced by a large window over-looking the lake gave Shawn's office a sense of opulence, much more ostentatious than my dad's office had been. The room had a large desk with ornately carved legs, a brown leather office chair, and a matching love seat on the wall with all of Shawn's awards. I felt my knees give a little when my gaze landed on the picture of my dad pinning a commendation award on Shawn's chest after his heroism during the floods of 1993. I had been sitting in the audience when Shawn had received the award. I remembered feeling so much pride.

I sighed. I'd loved him once upon a time.

There was a sturdy cushioned chair across from his desk. I sat down, crossing my legs, and waited for him to go around the desk to his chair.

"How have you been, Nora? I mean, since your mom..."

"I'm okay." I still had days where I wanted to throw things. Mom had been full of life and energy. She'd been the president of the historical society, she went dancing on Fridays at the senior center, and she played the piano every Wednesday night with a group of friends who liked to get together to jam, until she couldn't. If it hadn't been for the cancer...

I took a deep breath to steady myself. I'd worked really hard to deal with my grief these past six months, and I wouldn't let Shawn's show of sympathy raise a fresh fountain of sorrow in me.

I looked past my ex to the window ledge full of framed photos behind him. One was a woman with her arms wrapped around two small children. I assumed it was Shawn's wife, Leila, and their sons. Leila's blonde hair was straight, teased up and pulled back on top. She had a heart-shaped face, hazel eyes, a Miss America smile. I'd not met her or Shawn's sons before, but I could see he'd married a beauty.

Although, it wasn't a recent picture, because there were several pictures of the boys as they aged into handsome adults. One of them reminded me so much of

Shawn when he was young, and the other one had Leila's face shape, but Shawn's dad's mouth and nose. "You have a nice-looking family."

His cheeks pinked as he smiled. "Jacob just got his bachelor's degree in psychology from Kansas University, and Shawn, Jr., is getting ready to graduate from high school this year. He's in the running for valedictorian." He was bubbling with pride, and as much as I hadn't wanted kids, I was happy for him. "He was offered a baseball scholarship and an academic scholarship. He just needs to choose his path."

"It sounds like you raised two bright boys." There was a small wooden bat on a pedestal sitting on his desk. I couldn't read the plate without my glasses on, so I leaned in for a closer look. The words just got blurrier. I smelled pine and urethane, so it had to be a fairly new award.

"And the MVP goes to Shawn Rafferty," a man said. A sturdy teen pivots to face me. His face is fuzzy, and I wish I was wearing my glasses.

"Way to go, Shawnie," another man says. I recognize my ex's voice. "I'm proud of you."

"Thanks, Dad."

I watch the young man walk away, and I feel an overwhelming sense of accomplishment coming from Shawn.

"Your son got the MVP award for his team."

"Yes." Shawn smiled. I guess he assumed I could read the trophy. "He earned it."

"Congratulations." It seemed as if everything worked out the way it was supposed to. Shawn got the life he wanted. Two perfect sons and one perfect wife. I tapped my nails on his desk. "Can we get down to the reason you ordered me to come see you?"

"Of course." He nodded. "Look. I know how important your friendship is with Gilly. You two have always been peas in a pod. I also know that you are going to do everything you can to try and help her, just like the time she got caught with gin in her locker at school, and you tried to take the blame."

"This is nothing like that, Shawn. If I didn't believe Gilly was one-hundred percent innocent—"

Besides, I'd come up with the plan to spike the cafeteria's fruit punch. Gilly had only taken the bottle of gin from her dad's stash because I had thought it would be funny. In that instance, no matter how much I'd told the principal it was my doing, Gilly had taken the brunt of the punishment. She was given a five-day OSS, out-of-school suspension, while I, being the chief of police's daughter, was only given a one-day ISS, in-school suspension. Thank heavens we were teenagers in the eighties. We would have probably been kicked out of school permanently or something worse nowadays.

He cut me off. "I'm just giving you a heads up. If you interfere in this police investigation, I'll have no other choice than to come down hard on you, no matter our history."

Ancient history, I thought. The fact that my ex-husband acted like he still knew me got on my last nerve. His Nora intel was more than twenty years old, and him presuming I hadn't had any personal growth in the last two decades was insulting. I qualified for AARP, for goodness sake! "No worries, Shawn. I don't expect any favors from you."

His eyes narrowed, the creases between his brows deepening. "Good."

"You do realize that I'm the daughter of the man who held your job before you did. I know how the law works. Interference with police in this state only pertains to someone who resists arrest or tries to interfere with the arrest of someone else. That gives me a lot of latitude, so don't think for one second that I'll let Gilly go down for a crime she didn't commit. I can't believe she's in holding because she's the easy suspect."

"We're not trying to railroad her. You know that, don't you?"

"Nope," I said, earning another of his narrowed gazes. "Honestly, did you bring me down here to issue a personal warning?"

"No." He stood up. "I used to work with Lloyd when he was on the force. I read the report you filed against him."

"Okay," I said. "What of it?"

He shook his head. "You could have gotten yourself hurt. What in the world were you thinking, confronting him with a weapon?"

"Really? Just in case you've forgotten, my dad taught me how to shoot when I was thirteen. Hell, you and I used to go to the gun range at least once a month to keep my skills sharp." I still went a couple of times a year.

"You could've gotten yourself killed, Nora."

Irritated, I practically levitated from the chair. "I handled the situation, Shawn. What the hell do you want from me?"

"We have history, Nora. And even if we didn't, I owe it to your dad to look out for you if I can."

Of for the love of—*argh*! Lord save me from men who suffered from knight-in-shining-armor delusions. I spoke calmly but firmly. "That's a nice sentiment, Shawn. But, I'm not your concern anymore, and I haven't been for a very long time."

His lips thinned. "Understood. I guess there's nothing left to say then." He came around his desk, and when I stood up, I detected the aroma of pungent, woodsy cologne. And then...

A blonde woman with matted thinning hair and wearing loose gray pajamas, says, "I don't want you to worry about me, Shawn. I love you, but I'm not a China doll."

"Come on, Leila, the doctor says you need to take it easy. Especially now that you're getting the radiation treatments."

"And I am." She leans into the man, goes on up on her tiptoes, her blurry face skimming his in what I assume is a kiss. "You're wearing the Prism Specter cologne I got you for Christmas," she says. "I love the way it smells on you."

"I know," he says, his voice with just a hint of worry. "That's why I wear it."

"Oh," I stammered. Shawn's wife was sick? Could that be right? I shook my head. "I'm sorry, Shawn."

He misunderstood my apology. "It's fine, Nora. You're right. You're not my concern anymore. Thanks for coming down."

Cripes. I didn't want to add to his misery, and I couldn't exactly ask him about Leila. Or help him, for that matter. The only thing I could do right now was try to help Gilly.

"Can you tell me one thing? Did something happen when you worked with Lloyd that made him seem dangerous to you?" I'd bet every ounce of my five-hundred-dollars-an-ounce sandalwood oil that Lloyd had made enemies as a police officer. Those enemies, as far as I was concerned, were more viable suspects than my best friend.

"I'm not going to discuss an ongoing investigation with you, Nora."

"So, you are looking into other people?"

"I'm not going to—"

I raised my hand. "I get it. But does Lloyd's abusive behavior have anything to do with his early retirement from the GCPD? I heard he'd gotten in trouble with a woman he pulled over, and you all fired him as part of the settlement?"

His nostrils flared and he scowled. "I can't talk about that either."

"I'll take that as a yes."

"Take it however you want, Nora. Just take it somewhere else."

"How long had Lloyd been with GCPD before he took the job at the Rose Palace Resort?"

"In case you haven't noticed, I'm not going to answer any of your questions. Goodbye, Nora, and stay out of the investigation," he said as his parting words.

As the door closed between us, I checked my phone. It had been over an hour since Gilly had been brought in. I wondered if Shawn would have me arrested if I stormed the bullpen and raised a ruckus.

Well. I guess I was going to find out.

CHAPTER
NINE

Turned out, I couldn't access the bullpen without a key card. Unlike the old police station, where everything was accessible if you knew which doors to open, the new building had all kinds of security. I only had one option: sweet-talk information from the cop manning the front desk.

I was relieved to see Billy Simpson, who had to be getting close to retirement, behind the counter. My dad had hired him when he'd first graduated from the police academy. While most officers retired after twenty years, Billy had to be pushing thirty on the force. Even when my dad was alive, I'd never had to work the chief of police's daughter angle before, but I wasn't above pandering to find out just how bad things were for Gilly.

I straightened my shoulders and crossed the room to him. "Hi, Billy," I said. "How are you?"

He raised his bushy gray brows and frowned as he

peered at me through a pair of thick bifocals. "Can I help you?"

Shoot. The last time I'd seen Billy was at Dad's funeral, like most of the men and women on the force, so I'd been in my thirties at the time. The fact that he didn't recognize me ouched a little. So much for working a connection. "Uhm, a friend of mine was brought in earlier. Gillian Martin. Can I find out if she's been processed yet?"

He pushed his glasses up his nose and squinted at me. "Nora? Nora Rafferty?"

"Hey." I smiled. "It's Black now."

He grinned. "Oh, yeah, right. Sorry about that. Wow, you haven't changed a bit."

I chuckled because obviously I had, but it was nice of him to say. I struggled to recall more about Billy than employment history. "How's your wife?" I wished I could remember her name, but it eluded me.

"She's doing great. Just retired from the school district after twenty-five years."

"How nice. Are you planning to join her?"

He let out a loud belly laugh. "I retired five years ago and decided to come back part-time a few months ago. A good marriage requires some distance." He laughed again. "At least in our case. She's happy I'm not under her feet, and I'm happy to not have a honey-do list as long as my leg to work on. It is amazing how much stuff that woman can find to do around the house."

I could imagine. I was home for two months, and while I wasn't allowed to work, I had made my own honey-do list of items that needed upgraded or repaired. When you're staring at a splintered baseboard or a loose cupboard every day, all day long, there is a sense of urgency to get them fixed. Currently, though, I had bigger things on my to-do list than household chores. "Billy, I'd love to catch up with you some time, but I'm really worried about my friend."

"Oh, yes. Of course." He tapped on his computer keyboard to wake up his monitor then slid his glasses back down his nose a little before he poised his index finger over the J key. "Jill Barton, you said?"

"Gillian Martin," I corrected. "With a G." I pointed at the G key. "She was arrested about two hours ago."

After a painfully slow pecking, featuring lots of taps on the backspace key, Billy finally hit enter. "Ah." He nodded. "Here she is."

I leaned over to catch a glimpse. Billy didn't try to hide the screen. The picture that came up was awful. Gilly would absolutely be crushed to see that the angle had highlighted her double chin and created a weird neck roll.

"They haven't processed her completely." He leaned in closer, tilting his head back so he could get a better view through the reading part of his bifocals. "I'm afraid she's not going to be going anywhere tonight. She has a bond hearing in the morning." He grimaced. "But I wouldn't get my hopes up. The charges are serious, and bail is likely to be high."

What he didn't say was that, worst-case scenario,

the judge could deny Gilly bail. "What are the charges against her, exactly?"

"Second-degree murder."

"That's completely ridiculous!"

"I don't have a lot of information, since the arrest report hasn't been logged in, but I can say with a fair amount of certainty that Detective Holden wouldn't have taken your friend into custody without strong evidence."

My anxiety level ramped up. "Can I see her? Is there any way to get me back to holding? Is she even in holding? Has she asked for a lawyer?"

"I'm sorry, Nora. I can see you're upset, but I just don't have the answers to any of those questions."

A knock at the glass behind his desk drew our attention. It was Holden. He opened the door to the bullpen. "What are you doing here?" he asked.

"What do you think? I'm trying to find out what you all are doing with Gilly."

Holden rubbed his eyes. "Go home, Nora."

"Not until I see Gilly."

"Then I hope you brought a tent with you." He looked at Billy. "I'm going home. If Ms. Black gets too rowdy, you have my permission to arrest her."

Billy suddenly looked as if he swallowed a bug. "Uh, okay."

I glowered at Ezra. "You can't expect me to do nothing."

"While I don't expect it," he said, "I can certainly hope." He closed the door behind him and walked past me to the exit. He waved without looking back. "Good night, Billy."

"Night," Billy replied.

I stared at Billy, who avoided eye contact. "Thanks for your help," I said. It wasn't his fault that my friend was in jail and Detective Holden was an idiot.

"Good luck, Nora. Sorry about Jill."

I didn't bother correcting him. I turned on my heel and hurried out of the station. My knees protested every step of the way, so it was difficult for me to do much more than a fast walk. But the detective was tired, and I was motivated. I caught up to him before he could get into his truck.

I put my hand on the door.

His shoulders sagged as he shook his head. "I can't do this with you, Nora."

"Then you better arrest me, Ezra." Tears burned at the corners of my eyes. My voice choked. "I have to do something. She's my best friend. She's all the family I have left. Please."

He looked down at me, his tired eyes full of compassion. "Nora," he said softly.

"Please," I said again. "Help me." The sky had grayed in the past couple of hours, as if Mother Nature shared my misery. "If nothing else, help me to understand why you're so sure it's Gilly. That she did this."

"The knife in Lloyd's chest was a professional six-inch utility knife." He paused. "G and R are etched into its handle."

"So what?" I swallowed hard because I knew exactly

what that meant. When Gilly had divorced Gio Rossi, she'd kept his fancy knives—a Michel Bras set that cost him almost three thousand dollars. It was her final screw-you to her ex. He'd loved those knives, and when they were his, he'd treated them like precious jewels. Gilly, however, used them to slice open cardboard boxes and cut flowers. I rarely ever saw her use them on food. And never on people, for heaven's sake.

He eased my hand away from his door. "Your friend had the block of knives on display in her kitchen, in full view of my officers." He held up his hand to stop my protest. "I know what the arrest warrant said. And you probably know anything suspicious within view is up for grabs even if it's not listed on the warrant. The set was complete, except for—"

"The utility knife," I finished, suddenly numb to my toes.

"In case you want to question my due diligence," he said, his voice hoarse with exhaustion, "no one else in town owns, or has owned, a three-thousand-dollar Michel Bras knife set. And the former owner verified the utility knife was from the set."

"You tracked down Gilly's ex?"

"I'm good at my job, Nora." He unlocked the truck's door. "I haven't slept in almost two days, so I'm going home to get some rest. You can't do anything for Ms. Martin tonight, so you should do the same."

"It's only five o'clock," I told him. I mean, I was old, but I wasn't falling-asleep-at-seven-with-the-TV-on old. Well, most nights anyhow. "Besides, I have two scared teenagers I'm going to have to explain this all to, and since I can't even figure out how to make sense of today for myself, I have a feeling it's going to be an impossible task."

He gave me a sympathetic smile. "With teenagers, you just have to be direct and honest, and then let them sort it out. Don't expect them to react in a way you expect. And just be okay with whatever comes. They are going to need a lot of support from you."

"Do you have a lot of experience with teenagers?"

"Only one, Mason. He's sixteen now." Ezra shook his head and blew out a breath. "Three years of family counseling has taught me that kids are going to feel how they're going to feel, and nothing you say or do is going to change that. But the good news is, they usually come around."

That bit of information took me aback for a moment. "I thought you said you weren't married."

"I'm not," he said. "But I was. I moved here six years ago when my ex-wife remarried Roger Portman."

"The guy who owns Portman's on the Lake Resort? He's kind of old for her, right?"

"His son," Ezra said. "But he's in line to inherit the place. I had to give permission for her to move with our son. There was no convincing me at first, but when Mason asked me himself, I couldn't say no. Instead, I put in my application down here then put in my notice with the Springfield police department."

So, Ezra had moved to the area to be near his son.

"How did your ex-wife take you following her to Garden Cove?"

He chuckled. "Not well, but she adjusted, as we all do." He opened the door. "I really have to go or I'm going to fall asleep on the way home."

I nodded. "Stay safe, Ezra."

"You too, Nora."

I stepped back as he started his truck, reversed out of the spot, then drove off the parking lot. At least now I knew about the evidence against Gilly. The witness who had put her at the scene of the crime, and one of Gio's prize knives had killed Lloyd. Add to that Gilly's threat to end Lloyd, and it all started to look extremely damning.

The most logical place to start was with the Littles. Lloyd had gone there last night looking for Ricky Little, Rita's son. Maybe later that night, he'd found him. But how would Ricky have gotten Gilly's knife?

Damn it. I would not lose faith in my BFF. Someone jabbed that knife into Lloyd's chest, but it was not Gilly.

That was a tomorrow problem.

Tonight, I had to figure out how to tell two terrified sixteen-year-olds their mom had been arrested for murder.

CHAPTER
TEN

I swung by the shop to pick up the kids. Pippa offered to close up. Man, she was worth her weight and mine in gold, and I told her so.

The car ride home was somber. I'd offered to take the kids to dinner, but they shot down every food suggestion. They didn't even go for fast food—and I thought teenagers lived on hamburgers and Cokes. Well, I had a few ribs at the house, along with some frozen dinners. I hoped if they did get hungry, it would be enough.

"When are we going home?" Ari asked. She dropped her bomber jacket on the floor near my couch.

I picked it up and laid it over the banister. "Maybe tomorrow." I hoped, anyhow. It would all depend on the bond hearing. As long as the judge granted her bail, I would figure out a way to get Gilly home, even if I had to mortgage the house.

I'd explained to the siblings as much as I could about

their mom's arrest on the way to my house. Ari ranted for a bit then cried. Marco, always the opposite, grunted then played games on his phone all the way to my house.

"Don't worry," I said to them. "Your mom is innocent. She won't go to jail."

"Don't be naive, Aunt Nora," Ari said. "Innocent people go to jail every day. The penal system in this country doesn't care about justice, they care about convictions. Mom is just another number to them."

My heart began to pound in my chest. Christ, Ari was intense. It was hard to come up with the right words to calm her when I was having trouble talking myself down off the ledge. "Well, not in Garden Cove," I said lamely. "I'll make sure your mom doesn't get a bum rush."

Marco tapped his thumbs over the tiny keyboard on his phone. "A bum's rush is when you forcibly remove someone from somewhere."

I could have sworn it was bum something or another. "A bum steer?" I asked.

He tapped some more. "When someone gives you misinformation."

"You're being a bit of a bum-hole," I said. "I'm just saying, your mom is going to beat this rap." I snapped my fingers. "Bum rap," I said triumphantly.

Marco chuckled. "That's it."

"How can you two make jokes right now? Mom could be sent to prison for life. Murder two is not a laughing matter." Ari's mascara was not waterproof.

Between crying and rubbing, she looked as if she was turning into a raccoon.

"I'm sorry, Ari. I don't think it's funny. Not at all. But people are like teapots. You can sit on a cold stove forever without incident, but if someone turns up the heat, you have to let off some steam or you might explode." I gave her a quick hug that she didn't return. "You know I love your mom like she's my twin. I promise you that I'm not taking any of this lightly."

Ari nodded, then hiccupped.

"Why don't you take the spare room," I told her. "Marco, you're okay to sleep on the couch, right?"

He shrugged, already back to killing angry candy farm animals on his phone.

"Okay. That's settled then. I'll go find some sheets and blankets. If you guys get hungry, feel free to raid the fridge, freezer, and pantry. Drinks are in the garage fridge. All diet. I apologize for that, but it's what I drink."

I went up the stairs, holding on to the banister for support. My knees hurt less if I could use my arms to take some of the weight. When I got to my room, I closed the door behind me, sat on my bed, and started bawling.

After a few minutes—and one really snotty, blotchy face later—I went into my en suite bathroom and washed my face.

"Christ, Nora," I said, patting my cheeks with a cold cloth. "Pull yourself together." I'd lost my dad and my mom. I wouldn't—couldn't—lose Gilly, too. I needed her as much as she needed me. More, probably.

A knock on the bedroom door straightened my back. "Aunt Nora," Ari said. "Marco wants to know if he can have the ribs."

"Yes," I said loud enough for her to hear me. Then it dawned on me. Those were the last ribs I would ever get from the Bar-B-Q Pit. Ever.

I stopped myself short of sobbing again as I changed into my most comfortable pajamas. They were pink with brown trim and covered in poop emojis. A joke gift from Gilly, but the PJs turned out to be my favorite leisurewear. After, I got into my linen chest for bedding. I grabbed a blue fuzzy blanket and some gray sheets. These would work for the fold-out couch. I grabbed some extra pillows from my closet and fit them with matching cases then headed downstairs with the bundle right up to my eyeballs.

Halfway down the stairs, I nearly missed a step and dropped the bedding. One of the pillows tumbled all the way down to the landing. "A little help!" I hollered.

Ari and Marco both came out of the kitchen, Marco holding one of my prize baby back ribs as he chewed a mouthful of falling-off-the-bone heaven.

"Oh, shit," I heard him say as he raced back into the kitchen then came out with empty hands except for a paper towel he was using to clean his fingers.

I didn't care if he said the occasional cuss word, but his mother did, so I said, "Language."

"Sorry, Aunt Nora." He picked up the pillow and flung it over to the couch. Then he and Ari grabbed the rest of my load and took it into the living room.

I heard a muffled ring. I hustled to my purse and got to my phone as it chimed out again. I didn't recognize the number, and while I normally would have let it go to voicemail, today was not the day to miss important phone calls.

I answered. "Hello?"

"Are Marco and Ari okay?" It was Gilly.

"Gilly!" Marco and Ari rushed to my side. I nodded to them and said, "Yes, they're here at my house with me. They're standing right next to me. How are you calling? Did you get out?"

"No," she said. "I had some cash in my purse. They let me put it on a phone account to make calls. It's fifty cents a minute. I was lucky I had ten dollars on me. You know I never carry money around like that." She sounded as tired as I felt. "They patted me down, Nora." I could hear the sneer of contempt in her voice. "It was humiliating."

"I'm sorry, Gils. Have you talked to your lawyer?"

"Yes. His name is Jasper Riley." I heard her take a shuddering breath. "Mr. Riley says they have a strong circumstantial case against me. He thinks, because of Lloyd's reputation, the prosecuting attorney will probably offer me a deal."

"You can't take a deal," I told her. "You didn't do this, and a deal would mean pleading guilty."

"They have a strong case, and I don't have an alibi, Nora. A deal could be the difference between getting ten years in prison versus thirty, or worse, life without parole."

"I'm getting you a new flippin' lawyer," I told her. "Because, hell no."

"Nora."

"Don't," I said. "Your arraignment hearing is tomorrow, and they'll set bail. Promise me you won't take any deal until you talk to me about it first."

"I love you, Nora, but you're not a lawyer. Or a cop."

"Or a mother," I added. The defeat in her voice broke my heart. "Do you really want me to raise your children? I can't even keep houseplants alive." I looked at Ari and Marco, and their expressions echoed my sentiments.

There was silence for a few seconds, then Gilly said, "You have a point. Let me talk to my kids."

I handed Ari the phone. She pressed the speaker button. "Mom," she said. Her hand trembled. Marco put his hand under hers for support. She gave him a rare smile of thanks.

"Ari," Gilly said with some relief. "Where's your brother?"

"I'm here, too, Mom," he said.

"When are you coming home?" Ari asked. I could see the tears brimming her eyes again.

"I'm working on it," Gilly said. "I love you both. You know that, right?"

"I love you, too, Mom," Ari said.

"Love you," Marco added quickly.

"You two be good for your aunt Nora. She's not me, but she does love you, and she'll make sure you have clothes on your back, a roof over your head, and you don't starve to death."

"I don't know," said Marco. "You haven't seen her fridge."

"I'll go grocery shopping tomorrow," I said. I hoped I wouldn't have to provide the essentials for too long. "Besides, your mom will be home soon. I'll see you tomorrow, Gilly."

I left the twins and went into the kitchen to give the three of them a chance to speak. I found a package of tuna, some unexpired mayo, mustard, some hamburger dill slices, and half an onion in the fridge. I pulled them all out and set them on the counter to make tuna salad sandwiches. It wouldn't be ribs, but it was better than a poke in the eye.

"Aunt Nora," Ari yelled. "Pippa's here!"

I dusted breadcrumbs from my fingertips and washed my hands before heading into the living room.

Pippa hadn't come alone, and I was suddenly self-conscious about the fact that I'd taken off my makeup and put on my poopy PJs.

"Hey, Pip. Jordy." All six-foot-two of Jordy Hines was standing by my entertainment center. "If I had known we were having company, I would have dressed more appropriately." I gave Pippa a wide-eyed WTH stare.

She shrugged. "Jordy has some information about Lloyd. I thought you'd want to hear it."

I quickly forgot my vanity. "Yes, of course. Please, have a seat, both of you."

Pippa and Jordy sat on the couch. His knee casually touched hers. Oh my. It seemed Pippa had been holding out on me.

"So," I said. "Is Jordy actually an ex-undercover DEA agent?"

"I'm a what?" he asked.

"Nothing," Pippa said. "Just a little joke." Now it was her turn to give me a WTH stare. Served her right.

"What can you tell me about Lloyd?" I asked.

The big man's gaze went to the teens. "I'm not sure we should talk about it right now."

"I want to hear," Marco said.

"Same," his sister agreed.

"How bad is it?" I asked Jordy.

"On a scale of one to ten, I'd put it at a seven."

I nodded. "Bad enough." I looked at the twins. "Sorry, guys."

"This is bull," Marco said, along with several more choice words, as he stormed out of the room. Ari trailed after him.

"You know they'll just listen at the door," Pippa said.

"Let's go outside," I told them.

Jordy popped up from the couch, then took Pippa's hand to help her up.

Once we put on coats, and I slipped on my fuzzy boots, we went out to the end of my driveway. Far enough to keep teenaged ears from eavesdropping.

"Okay, what do you know?"

Jordy frowned down at me. "Pippa told me Lloyd showed up at your place the other night looking for Gilly. She isn't the first woman Lloyd got stalkery with."

"I figured that was the case," I said. "Do you know who else he did this to?"

"From what I've heard, Ellen Brown is one of them. She works at the bank as Hal Brashears' assistant. She and Lloyd went out a few times when he was still a cop, and when she called it quits, he started following her, even when he was on duty. He stopped her on a bogus traffic violation, and when he made her get out of the car, he got rough. His partner at the time backed up Ellen's side of the story."

"Who was his partner?" I asked.

"I'm not sure," Jordy said, "but it seems it wouldn't be too hard to find out. I could ask around for you. I get police in the coffee shop every day."

I nodded. "That would be great. Anything else?"

"Yeah, I heard he was doing some enforcing on the side. I can't say if it's one-hundred-percent true, but someone said that Lloyd was collecting debts for a local bookie out of the Rose Palace Resort."

There was no legal gambling in Garden Cove. "Could that have been why he was looking for Ricky Little?" If he'd come to the restaurant to collect a debt, he hadn't exactly been circumspect about it. Of course, he'd also been drunk. I wonder what his bookie boss thought about that?

"Maybe," Jordy said. "I think it might be worth it for the police to look into it."

"You should tell Ezra Holden about this."

"Uh-uh," Jordy said, shaking his head. "It can't come from me. People treat me like a bartender or a therapist and tell me stuff they wouldn't say to most people. That'll stop if word gets around I'm sharing information with the police. Besides, some of it comes from officers who come in, so..."

"I get it. Barista-client confidentiality."

He gave me a half grin. "You're adorable."

"I'm too old to be adorable," I joked.

"You're not that old," he said.

"I'm fifty-one," I protested.

"I wouldn't have guessed it," Jordy said. "But considering my uncle turned one-hundred and three on his last birthday, seems to me, that makes you exactly middle-aged."

I chuckled. "I'll take it." I sniffed as a sweet scent caught my attention. "Do you smell vanilla?"

"That's me," Jordy said. "I spilled syrup on me earlier."

A large tattooed man lifts a woman whose haircut I recognize up onto a counter. I can't see their faces, but it's not hard to infer that they're making out. I also recognize the space where they're at. It's the workroom in the back of my shop. Pippa's hand slides back and she knocks a bottle of fragrance oil to the floor.

"Crap," she says. "That was one of Nora's Madagascar vanilla. She's going to kill me."

"I'll pay to replace it," Jordy says.

"Not my Madagascar vanilla oil." My lip jutted in a pout. That oil wasn't cheap, and it took weeks to get in an order.

"How did you know?" Gilly asked.

I tapped my nose. "My ability to distinguish scents is

highly evolved." That and the sexy-time vision I'd just had.

"It's my fault," Jordy said. "Pippa was showing me around, and I accidentally knocked it over."

"No worries," I said, rolling my gaze over to Pip. "Accidents happen."

When Jordy got in his car, I walked Pippa around to the passenger side. "I like you with Jordy. I think he's a keeper."

"I like him with me, too." She gave me a gentle elbow. "And I think you might be right."

After they left, I resisted the urge to track down Ezra and bash him over the head with information that I was certain he was already aware of. Had he been investigating Lloyd over the illegal gambling stuff? Had he been fishing for a bigger prize? Because that could have gotten Lloyd killed as well. Unfortunately, it didn't explain Gilly's knife used as the murder weapon.

Ezra told me he was good at his job.

Well, I needed him to be better. I was not letting my best friend take the fall for murder. And since I knew in my heart of hearts that Gilly didn't stab Lloyd, I was left with a bone-chilling realization.

The killer was still out there.

CHAPTER

ELEVEN

T he next morning, I stood in the shower and groaned as the jets beat hot water against my aching muscles. Man, I either needed to book a massage or to get laid. Getting laid was not happening anytime soon, so I made a mental note to book an appointment with my masseuse.

Gilly's hearing wasn't until ten, so the first thing I had planned this morning was to harangue Ezra Holden until he came around to my point of view. I hadn't moved my way up the ranks to regional sales manager of a top-tier beauty supply distributor because I wasn't persuasive. I could sell water to a shark if I put my mind to it. Besides, if he knew Gilly like I did, he would be turning over every rock and leaf in this town for the real killer. But since he didn't and wouldn't, I would have to do it myself.

The fact that I had some leads for other suspects had given me hope for a light at the end of this scary, life-without-parole tunnel. I wondered if the weird visions I'd been having might show me something that could help my friend. So far, other than the ones I'd had about Lloyd and Shawn's wife, the memories I'd tapped into were happy moments.

But they had all seemed tied to feelings. Maybe strong emotion was the key. If I found the actual murderer, if the feeling behind their actions was powerful enough, could I get a scent memory from them? Or, even better, how they got Gilly's knife and used it to kill Lloyd? Of course, all the visions had been tied to scents, as well. Could I manufacture an aroma to trigger the killer? So many theories and no murderers to practice on. Yet.

I turned off the water and stepped out of the shower, careful to place my foot on the bathmat. I'd had a pedicure and an eyebrow and lip wax on Friday after my doctor's appointment. I'd gone eight weeks without doing any beauty maintenance, and I had started to resemble the bearded lady. Okay, I didn't have that much hair on my face, but still. Every time the whiskers showed up, it was traumatic. Because of the pedicure, the bottoms of my feet were still slick when wet. I'd slid on the tile once already this weekend and strained my groin. I walked funny that entire day. I wouldn't make that mistake twice.

When I was suddenly confronted with Ari standing in front of me, I yelped and reached back to brace myself.

The teen looked appalled. "Good God, Aunt Nora, put on a towel," she said with a fair amount of dismay.

I was already stumbling back into the shower. Then I slipped on the wet shower stall. An unpleasant bellow escaped me as I collapsed to the stall floor like a shaken soufflé. "What are you doing in here?" I asked through gritted teeth.

"Uh. Sorry. Are you okay?" Ari asked from the other side of the curtain.

That seemed to be the question of the week. I could hear the worry in Ari's voice, but she didn't yank the curtain back to check on me. I didn't blame her. Right now, I didn't want to see me.

"Should I call nine-one-one?" she yelled.

"I'm not deaf," I yelled back. "Don't you dare call emergency services. Or you'll be the one in the back of that ambulance." I grabbed the bar in the stall and pulled myself up. My knees were banged up, and I'd hit my elbow against the hot water knob, but otherwise, I would survive. And bonus, there were no broken bones or strains. "What are you doing in here, Ari? This is my bathroom."

"You only have one other bathroom, Aunt Nora, and Marco is using it. I have to get ready for school." I'd given the twins the option to go to school or stay home. Both, still mad at me for leaving them out of the conversation the night before, opted to go to school.

Marco said he didn't want to lose his starting position as a third baseman on Friday, and if he missed more than one practice during the week, the coach would bench him for the first three innings. Ari's excuse was that she had a test in biochemistry, and she didn't want to ruin her GPA. I was fairly certain the coach and the biochem teacher would have understood if the kids skipped today, but I didn't argue. Instead, I washed the clothes they'd worn over to my house so they would be clean enough to wear again.

I'd ask the police if I could take them home after school today to get some clothes and daily essentials packed. I'd had several toothbrushes that I'd gotten from the dentist, so I had them covered in that department. They would have to wear the same underwear, because neither of them wanted to give them up last night. Ah well, one-day-old underwear wasn't going to hurt them.

"Besides," Ari said. "I didn't think you'd mind if I just came in to brush my teeth. I was going to wait but I'm not sure who takes longer showers, you or Marco."

The implications were yucky, at least where Marco was concerned. I hoped he wasn't masturbating in my guest bathroom, but I supposed it was better in there than on my couch.

Lord, save me from teenagers.

I reached out from behind the curtain. "Hand me a towel." I waited until I felt the plush terrycloth hit my palm then yanked it inside the shower and wrapped the towel around me.

When I stepped out again, I said, "Next time, wait your turn."

The ballsy kid stuck her tongue out at me. "What's for breakfast?" she asked.

"You just made me fall and now you want me to fix you breakfast?"

"I didn't make you fall," she said. "And besides, you're fine. Right? It's not like you broke a hip." She hesitated, concern crowding her gaze. "You didn't, did you?"

"No. Which is why I'm standing up on both legs, kid." Actually, I was closing in on the hip-breaking age every year, but I'd be damned if I'd admit it. "I can whip up some oatmeal for you and Marco."

Ari groaned. "Gross."

That did it. I unwrapped my towel and shook myself to the tune of "Ewww!" as Ari turned away. I rolled the terry cloth on the long fold and snapped my goddaughter right on the hip. The damp towel made a satisfying crack as it connected.

Ari jumped, then giggled, and that joyous sound, after all the girl had been through the last twenty-four hours, had been worth every bruise forming from the fall.

Ari had shut the door between us, so I dressed quickly and headed downstairs. My hair was shoulder length and curly when I let it dry naturally, something I rarely did.

Of course, the color, a deep golden brown, was something I did myself at home. Don't get me wrong, I used professional hair color, low ammonia, perfect for covering gray. I just liked to do it myself. When I worked in the city, a close friend had been a hairdresser. I'd given him discounts on our hair products, and he'd taught me how to color my own locks salon-style. Every six weeks, I was thankful for his tutelage. In between coloring, I used a touch-up gel on my roots. No one ever saw my grays. Not even Gilly.

My mother used to be the same way about her hair, until she'd lost most of it by the end of her illness. I'd bought her some fabulous real hair wigs. I still had some great connections in beauty supply, and a pal of mine had hooked me up with all of the wigs at wholesale. Mom's favorite had been a warm blonde with golden highlights and copper lowlights.

She'd said she loved that it made her look vibrant, even when she didn't feel it.

As vain as I was about my hair, I would have grown out the gray in a heartbeat if it had meant I could've spent one more day with Mom.

The world didn't work that way, though, and no amount of me "claiming my age" was going to bring her back.

The twins ate the oatmeal without too much complaint. I'd added some sugar, peach slices I'd had in the freezer, a dash of cinnamon, and lots of butter. And then it was time to get them to school. Jiminy Christmas. It was only seven in the morning, and I felt as if I'd run a marathon. Did Gilly do this every day? I'd always thought of my friend as a bit of a flake when it came to her personal life, but this parenting stuff was hard work. How did Gilly make it look so easy?

It was still chilly out, but signs of spring were everywhere. The grass had finally started to green out. Wild purple snow crocuses had cropped up overnight to pepper the lawn. I loved wildflowers. They knew how to live uncaged. The surprise lilies by my mailbox were starting to come up, which meant they looked like tall blades of thick grass. They were named surprise lilies because they didn't bloom until after the leaves all died. Until then, they just looked unremarkable. Mom always called them naked ladies. She said that every year they had to shed their clothes so they could shake their assets in front of the world. The memory made me smile.

I dropped the twins off at school then headed to the Bar-B-Q Pit. Rita and Nancy lived in a double-wide mobile home on the same property as the restaurant, but the two structures hadn't been built next to each other. Even so, it was a relief to see their home intact. I'd seen a trailer once that had burned until nothing was left but the metal frame it sat on. The family who had lived there had lost everything but their lives.

I pulled into the parking lot of the Pit. The roof, what I could see of it, had scorched holes in several places. The front door and the windows were boarded up. I'm sure that was one of the first things they did to keep people out. I hoped they were able to salvage any food they'd kept in the freezers.

The acrid smell of burned wood, metal, and plastic, along with the heaviness of hickory smoke, burned my nostrils and turned my stomach as I walked the perimeter. As I passed the dumpster around back, I got a strong whiff of trash—a mix of food and decay.

Someone is dragging something along the ground. They stop near the dumpster and lift the lid. The thing being dragged is large. It has feet. Dear Lord, it's a body. The knife sticking out of the chest confirms that it's probably Lloyd. It's dark, even with the streetlamp nearby, and the killer is wearing an oversized hooded sweatshirt.

The person, I'm pretty sure, is a man, the way they drag the body without too much difficulty, lower the lids, then drag the victim past the dumpster to a large round barrel on a stand.

"What are you doing, Nora?"

I spun around to face Detective Holden. "Uhm." I felt disoriented. Before the vision had started, I had been on the opposite side of the dumpster. Now I was a good ten feet past it and standing in front of a large metal barrel on metal legs. "I..."

He narrowed his green gaze and gave me a suspicious once over. "You got something to tell me, Nora?"

"What?" Had he somehow figured out my strange ability?

His expression was flat and cold. I'd never seen that look on his face before and it freaked me out. The fight-or-flight response vibrated right through me.

"Did you help Gilly Martin dispose of Briscoll?"

I felt the blood drain from my face. "No! No one disposed of anything. Or anyone."

Ezra stepped forward, his hand going to his gun hip, his voice low. "Oh, really? Then explain to me how you know that Briscoll's body was tossed into the smoker."

"What?" The shock of what he said rocked me to my core. "Someone put Lloyd in the smoker?"

That cinched it.

I was never eating barbeque again.

CHAPTER
TWELVE

I was acutely aware of Ezra's arm around me as he ushered me to the front of the parking lot. I wanted to protest, but I wasn't sure I could walk on my own. The news that Lloyd had been put inside the smoker had triggered another dizzy spell. I couldn't get the image out of my head of his dead body being dragged past the dumpster. I'd seen it, and I knew it was real. But this was the first time I'd had a vision without it being attached to a person.

How was that possible? I felt as if I were missing something huge, but I just couldn't quite put my finger on it. Or in this case, my olfactory senses. I really needed to figure out how my scent ability worked.

"I saw Lloyd being dragged toward the—" I gagged before I could finish my sentence.

Ezra stopped and turned me to face him. "Were you here when it happened? Is this a confession?"

"No," I sputtered. "Absolutely not."

"Then how could you know? Because that was the one item we held back from the press. Did you coerce Billy into telling you?"

"First, I'm pretty sure Billy doesn't know much. The reports hadn't even been written up when I was there yesterday. And second, why keep this a secret? Unless Lloyd died from being cooked and not kabobbed."

I wasn't trying to be funny, but Ezra cracked a smile. "You sure know how to paint a picture."

"Well, I just mean, if it wasn't the knife that killed him, then maybe—"

"It was the knife, Nora. He had two wounds. One to the stomach that the medical examiner says happened shortly before the killing blow to the chest."

"So not smoked?"

"Not a hint of smoke in his lungs. He was already dead by the time the killer put him in there."

I raised my brows. "Ah-ha! You said killer, not Gilly. Does this mean you're coming around to my way of thinking?"

"Not exactly," Ezra said. "I just don't want another lecture about your pal's innocence."

"But you're not one-hundred-percent certain she's guilty, right?" I asked hopefully.

"I'd say there's a ten-percent chance it might not be her."

"Those are terrible odds." I frowned. "What is it going to take for you to start looking at other suspects?"

"New evidence? Of course, you can tell me what you meant about seeing Lloyd's body being dragged."

Could I tell Ezra about my visions? Would he even believe me? I mean, it was happening to me, and I was having trouble wrapping my head around the phenomenon. What if this was hallucinations brought on by a hormonal imbalance coupled with a midlife crisis? Was the stuff I was seeing accurate? In some instances, absolutely, but maybe my brain was inferring things from the smells and offering up delusions as a way to make sense of the information. I didn't think I was clinically insane, but insane people never think they're crazy.

I decided to test Ezra with the vision I'd had of him as a child with his mother.

"Does your mother call you Easy-Peasy?"

He pursed his lips at me, then tilted his head. "My friends call me Easy."

I'd noticed that much. "Why?"

"My first name is Ezra. The first two letters are E and Z. It's not a stretch."

Duh, Nora. "But your mom, she called you Easy-Peasy, right?"

He looked away for a moment, a pained expression on his face. "Yes, but I don't know what that has to do with anything."

"I had surgery in mid-January."

"That's what your friend said the other night. Anything serious?"

"Serious enough." I didn't want to get into a deep conversation about my reproductive organs, or lack thereof. "I died during surgery. The doctor said I was gone for twenty-seven seconds before they were able to revive me."

Ezra's mouth opened then snapped shut. He focused his gaze on me, his nose twitching. "You're okay, though, now. Right?"

"No brain damage," I said. Although, maybe my hallucinations were a side effect of my temporary demise. I gave a slight head shake, then weighed out the pros and cons of confiding in the detective. The pros, he could believe me, and we could get down to the bottom of the real killer. The cons, he could believe I'd lost my mind and have me declared unfit to keep the twins while Gilly was prosecuted for murder.

I decided to take a chance. "Did your mother have a purple sweater with a scoop neck?"

"What? I...maybe. Look, my mother..." His expression was pained as he shook his head. "I don't like to talk about her."

"Oh." Well, shoot. Did I press him further, or did I risk his ire more by bringing up past grief? I did neither. Instead, I pivoted. Because I understood loss. "My mom passed away six months ago." My chest ached saying it aloud. I would have mentioned losing my father as well, which I'm sure he was well aware of since he'd told me he'd heard of him, but I wasn't trying to turn this into a my-sorrow-is-worse-than-yours kind of thing. All grief sucked. "I'm so sorry about your mom."

"It's not like that. She—" He let out a scratchy chuckle. "Now that I think of it, she did have a purple sweater. It had an animal on the front, but I can't recall exactly what it was."

"A penguin," I said.

"Yes! An emperor penguin. That's a pretty good guess." He blinked and then took a deep breath. "Are you going to tell me where this walk down memory lane is leading?" he asked. "Why all the questions about my mother and her choice of clothing? What the hell does this have to do with Lloyd's murder?"

"Okay. Well...since my surgery, I...uh." I cleared my throat. Wow. Admitting I had scent-related visions was more difficult than I thought. "You ever hear about how scent memory is the strongest?"

"Yeah. Sure." The furrow of his brow deepened. "And?"

"So, I have that. Scents bring on strong memories, except they're not mine."

He studied me for a moment, and I wondered if he was thinking about putting me on a psych hold. "You think your sense of smell is a kind of psychic power?"

The disbelief in his voice didn't bode well for me.

"Remember when you told me jasmine was your mom's favorite scent?"

"It was only a couple of days ago, so yeah."

"I got a vision of a little boy with green eyes. His mother said, 'Look at the flowers. Don't they smell good?' Then she picked him up and asked him to give her a smack. She patted her cheek. He kissed her. After, she called him Easy-Peasy. Her Easy-Peasy. I'm pretty sure that boy was you."

"I think you could extrapolate easy-peasy from my nickname. The rest is a guess. I've had psychics try to cold-read me before, Nora."

"I didn't know your nickname was Easy until after the vision."

He shook his head. "You know this is a hard pill to swallow, don't you?"

"I do."

"Okay, I'm not sure I'm buying all of this, but tell me what you think you saw behind the Pit."

"Every time I get one of these flashes of memory, it always has something to do with scent. I think the dumpster odor might have triggered the one about the killer. I couldn't really see him."

"Or her," Ezra said.

"Or her," I amended with a glare. "But he or she was dragging Lloyd across the asphalt toward the smoker."

"And you could see Lloyd's face?"

Whoops. I hadn't told him about that part. "I can't make out faces in the visions. They're always blurry. I can see hair, clothes, and other stuff, but no face."

"Then what makes you think this killer was dragging Briscoll's body?"

"Because I could see the knife in his chest."

Ezra rubbed his hand over his mouth and then scratched his head. "Do you think if you were back by the dumpster again, you might see more?"

"I don't know. Maybe." Well, so far so good. He hadn't called in for backup, and he'd offered a helpful suggestion.

Or maybe he's trying to trick you into incriminating yourself, stupid.

I pushed away the voice of doubt. I had a lot to gain if I could convince Ezra to take me seriously. "I'm willing to give it a try."

THIRTEEN

I'd been sniffing the air like a bloodhound on a desperate trail for several minutes, without any result. What was it my mother always said? Children and pets will make fools of you every time. She had been referring to the time I learned to play "Für Elise" on the keyboard when I was thirteen, but when she prodded me to play for her friends, the song had sounded more like a mangled, out-of-key version of "Chopsticks".

It turned out that trying to use this new psychic gift —or rather, curse, since it was making me look like a complete fraud—fell into that same category.

I paced back and forth between the dumpster and the smoker, and while the odor was bad, it wasn't triggering.

A loud clang, then the wet, rancid smell of dying vegetables and spoiled meat churned up the air around me, and I staggered as I looked back at Ezra, who had flung open the dumpster lid.

"You said you needed the smell," he said.

I gagged. "I don't think it's going to wor—"

A man in a hooded sweatshirt tows a figure across the pavement. I see a knife in the body's chest. It has to be Lloyd. The man stops in front of the dumpster. He opens the lid, the rotten smell makes him lean back away from the opening. Is there something in his other hand?

I can't tell because shadows are cutting into his form and making it difficult to make out details.

He puts his hand inside then withdraws it, dropping the cover with a clang. After, he goes back to Lloyd and hauls him toward the smoker.

"Nora," Ezra said. He held me by the arms again, holding me steady. "Nora?"

"I'm okay," I said breathlessly.

"It looked like you were having a focal seizure. Just completely zoned out. Are you sure you feel all right?"

I nodded. "I saw something I missed the first time."

He gave his lower lip a worried tug with his teeth, but then said, "Tell me."

"I think the killer either dropped something into the dumpster or he took something out."

"Could you tell for sure it was a man?"

"I'm ninety percent certain," I told him, reversing his earlier numbers about Gilly's possible innocence. "He had the build of a guy. Big shoulders. Tall. He was wearing a hooded sweatshirt, so I couldn't see his face or his hair."

"Okay. But Nora, scent-induced visions aren't evidence. I'm not even sure they're real." He found a small, empty wooden crate near the back door of the restaurant. He put it next to the dumpster then stepped up on it. He peered into the trash container. "I'm not seeing anything except regular garbage."

"Dig around."

He pinched the bridge of his nose and leaned farther over the ledge. "Nope," he finally said. "Not without gloves."

"Maybe check the other side," I directed.

Ezra flattened me with a stare. "Are you messing with me? I swear to God, Nora—"

"I'm not messing with you. Honest!"

He got down and moved the crate to the far-left corner. Again, he stepped up and looked inside. The emotions that played on his face went from annoyance, to disgust, then finally to surprise and disbelief. "See if you can find something to poke around in here. A stick maybe."

"What do you see?"

"Not sure," he said.

I found a piece of rusted rebar by the smoker and brought it back to him. "Will this do?"

He took it then poked around in the tall bin for a few seconds. He grunted then threw the rebar onto the ground next to the dumpster.

"Don't leave me in suspense here? What did you find?"

"A brick of cash."

I hurried to get up next to him, put my foot on the corner of the crate and stepped up to peek over. Ezra gave me a bemused look but didn't stop me. To the contrary, he put his arm around my waist to help me balance, then pointed to a plastic-wrapped bundle near a glob of trimmed beef fat.

"Yuck."

"I can make out that the top bill is a hundred. If the whole stack, which looks to be about an inch thick, is all hundreds, that's probably around ten grand in cash."

I whistled. "That's a chunk of change."

He nodded. "But why throw it in the trash?"

"When is trash day?" I asked.

"I'm not sure," Ezra replied. "You think the person who put it in here might work for the waste and disposal?"

"Possibly, or the guy threw it in here to hide it for some reason. Maybe he planned to come back and retrieve it later."

"But why not take it with him?"

"Hah! You said him."

"Only so we can keep this conversation moving," Ezra admitted. Though secretly, I thought he was having some strong doubts about Gilly being the murderer, and I counted that as serious progress.

"Look, Gilly swears she went straight home after picking up her car. What witness said they saw her vehicle here?"

"You know I can't tell you that, Nora." He looked at his watch again. "It's after nine. If you want to make your friend's bond hearing, you should go now."

"What are you going to do?"

"I'm going to get a crime scene investigator out here to retrieve the money and see if there are any other pieces of evidence we missed yesterday."

I turned my head to look up at him. Our faces were only inches apart. "So, you're willing to look at other suspects?" I asked breathlessly.

He gave a slight shake of his head. "Officially, Gilly has been charged. I can't investigate for a different suspect when we have someone already on the hook. I will have to treat this like a separate case."

"Unofficially?"

His green eyes smoldered as he gave me a look that sizzled me to my toes. "Unofficially, I'm going to look at more suspects." A curl of his sandy-brown hair fell onto his forehead. I reached up with my index finger and slid it back up into place.

Ezra licked his slightly bowed lips, his gaze unwaveringly on my mouth.

My hand slipped off the dumpster ledge, my fingers landing in something wet. Ew! And the never-ending scent of *Eau de Garbage* reeled at my senses, starting with my common sense. I swallowed the lump in my throat. "I better go." Gilly needed me, and that had to be my one and only focus.

"Can I call you?"

"When?" I asked.

"Tonight," he said. "Maybe we can test out this Smell-O-Vision of yours some more."

I smirked. "You're not old enough to know about Smell-O-Vision."

"You'd be surprised what I'm old enough to know."

Eeep! My instincts said to run away but my libido said, "We'll see about that. Call me tonight." Then I added, "So, you can tell me what you learn about the brick of money, of course."

He helped me down from the crate. "Of course," he agreed.

———

I DROVE FASTER than the speed limit on my way to the courthouse and found a place to park. Garden Cove wasn't a tiny town, but it wasn't so big that I had to fight a crowd to get a seat in the courtroom. Gilly was sitting in the front row, her shoulders hunched, with three other women who all looked as unhappy as my friend.

I moved up the aisle to get as close to her as I could. "Gilly!" I hissed.

She turned around, her pale cheeks pinking when she saw me.

"Don't give up hope," I said in a hushed but clear voice. "I think I found a lead."

Her shoulders straightened.

"Move away from the defendants," the bailiff said.

I gave the rotund man a scathing glare.

He patted his side piece. "I can have you removed."

Well, damn and double damn. I raised my hands. "I'm moving back." I turned my attention back to Gilly. "Don't give up hope," I told her. "Because I'm not going to stop fighting for you."

She smiled, sad and sweet. "I know you won't."

"Don't make me tell you again, miss," the bailiff said.

"I'm going," I said.

I saw Mr. Garner, Gilly's neighbor, sitting a few rows back. There was some space next to him on the bench. "Can I sit by you?" I asked.

He scooted over. "Certainly."

"All rise. The honorable Judge Randall Watson presiding," the bailiff said, bringing the court to order.

Mr. Garner and I stood up together.

The judge, an older man in his sixties, with gray hair, a weirdly dark mustache, and thick glasses, waddled up to take his place behind his bench. "Have a seat," he told us. "Let's get this moving along. First on the docket is Gillian Marie Martin. Is she in the courtroom today?"

A thin man with a beak of a nose sat at a desk in front of Gilly. He turned to her and gestured for her to get up. She did. "I'm Gillian Martin, your honor," she said. Gilly was such a gregarious person, but right then her voice sounded small and timid. It made my heart hurt.

"Charges," the judge said.

A woman, her hair pulled back in a severe bun, wearing glasses that you might see on an elderly librarian, stood up from a desk on the other side of the aisle and said, "Jessica Lyons for the prosecution, your honor. Ms. Martin is being charged with second-degree murder in the unlawful death of Mr. Lloyd Briscoll." Ms. Lyons appeared competent and unflappable. Not going to lie, it made me nervous.

"Defense," the judge said.

"Jasper Riley for the defense." The lawyer reminded me of a well-dressed Ichabod Crane, all legs, arms, and nose. He didn't look like a happy man. It made me even more determined to find someone better to defend my friend. "We asked the defendant be released on bail. She has strong ties to the community. She has been a resident her entire life. She is a single parent to two teenage children and is therefore not a flight risk. She has no criminal record and does not in any way pose a risk to the community. We ask that Ms. Martin be released on her own recognizance."

The judge turned his attention to Ms. Lyons. "Prosecution?"

"The prosecution asks that Bail be set at two-hundred and fifty thousand dollars, and we ask that Ms. Martin's movements be restricted to that of her home and work until the arraignment hearing."

The judge raised a bushy brow. "Mr. Riley?"

Ichabod Lawyer sighed. "Two hundred and fifty thousand would be a hardship for my client, your honor. We request that bail be lowered at this time."

"How much?" the judge asked.

"My client has assets of seventy-five thousand."

The judge turned to the prosecutor. "Ms. Lyons?"

She pushed her glasses up and rubbed the bridge of her nose. "It's low," she said, "But I am in agreement with Mr. Riley that Ms. Martin isn't a danger or risk to the community. I will allow the lower bail amount."

I didn't know who looked more surprised, Gilly, her lawyer, or the judge.

Judge Watson flipped through Gilly's file, or at least that was my assumption, before clearing his throat to get the court's attention. "I don't find sufficient reason to deny Gillian Martin bail at this time." He leaned forward and gave Gilly a scowl. "Young lady, the charges against you are very serious. Do you understand?"

Gilly's lower lip trembled. "Yes, your honor."

He nodded. "Bail granted in the amount of seventy-five thousand dollars."

There was a collective sigh of relief from Mr. Garner and me. He'd been on the edge of his seat as much as I had. "She's getting out," I said, almost giddy. I could admit to myself now that I'd been worried Gilly wouldn't be granted bail at all.

Mr. Garner smiled at me. "Gilly's such a good neighbor. I'm glad she's coming home."

I patted his arm then got up and into the aisle as Jasper Riley made his way toward the exit. "Hey," I said. "How soon will Gilly be released?"

"As soon as her bail is paid," he said brusquely. He paused and stared at me. "Make sure she doesn't skip town." Then off he went, all gangly and self-righteous.

What a dick.

I was definitely getting my BFF a new lawyer.

Just as soon as I traded my life savings for her freedom.

And after that?

I was gonna catch a killer. No matter what it took.

FOURTEEN

When Gilly exited the courthouse, I gave her the most spine-cracking hug I could muster. She looked worn down, her hair dull and her eyes red.

I ran my fingertips through the ends of her hair. "If one night in city jail takes this kind of toll on you, prison is going to turn you into a beast," I teased.

Gilly thinned her lips. "That's not funny, Nora. If it weren't for the kids, I'd seriously consider running right now. That was the most awful night of my life, and I was married to Gio Rossi for nine years."

I put my arm around her as we made our way to my car. "Speaking of Gio, how in the world did his knife end up in Lloyd?"

"I have no clue. You know I don't even use those knives to cook."

"That's because you don't cook."

"Only when I have to." She tapped her chin. "I think

the last time I used one was in the fall when I cut back the rose bush on the side of the house."

"We'll figure it out," I said more confidently than I felt. I used my key fob to unlock the car doors as we got close. "Home first?"

We split up and Gilly walked to the passenger door. "The police impounded my car to search it for evidence. Can you drive me out to the Rose Palace? I need to talk to Phil." Phil Williams ran the Rose Palace Resort. He was the one who had promoted Gilly to spa manager. "The terms of my bail require me to be employed." She rubbed her arms. "I need to check in with Phil to make sure I still have a job."

"You've given that place over twenty years of your life, babe. Surely, they won't fire you."

"I hope not." She got in on her side and I got in on mine. "But Lloyd worked there, too. If they think—"

"Only a fool would think you did this." When she didn't respond back, I asked, "Do you want to go shower and change first?"

Gilly shook her head. "No. Once I get home, I just want to be home, you know? I'm so tired, Nora. I just want this nightmare over with."

"Can you call Phil instead?"

"I need to look him in the eye, Nora. People find it more difficult to give bad news if you're looking them in the eye."

"True." I put the car in gear. "Okay, resort first. Taco Shake Shack second, and then home." Taco Shake Shack had been around since we were teenagers and had the nastiest, most delicious, artery-clogging deep-fried tacos. It was still cheap eats, too. For five bucks you got three tacos and a small shake.

Gilly's smile didn't reach her eyes. "That sounds good. Thanks, Nora."

"That's what friends are for." I drove out of the courthouse parking lot, pulled onto Marigold Street, and headed south toward the Rose Palace Resort. I wondered if I could get into Lloyd's office. There might be a clue to who might have killed him and why. Maybe a co-worker, or the security guards he bossed around, might know. I didn't relish the idea of trying to trigger a vision again, but for Gilly, I would sniff every single person at the resort if it meant she wouldn't ever see the inside of a cell again.

"How are Marco and Ari?" she asked.

"Surprisingly okay," I said. "They both decided to go to school today."

"Sounds about right," Gilly said. "I've told you how Ari is about her grades. I worry sometimes that she's too fixed on being perfect when it comes to school. She got an A minus on a calculus test in ninth grade, and she wouldn't eat the next day. She cried for two nights. She saw a counselor for a while, and she basically said that Ari has abandonment issues thanks to her dad. And that grades are an area of her life she can control. So, her going to school makes perfect sense to me."

Now that Gilly had explained it, it made more sense to me as well. "Marco wanted to go so he wouldn't get benched for three innings. He said he couldn't miss another practice."

Gilly sighed. "If I know Marco, he went to school because his sister did. I see his kindness, especially in the way that he supports Ari when he isn't worried about looking weak."

I remembered him supporting his sister's hand when she held the phone the night before. I nodded. "I see that in him." His dad leaving did a number on him, too.

"Ari is better at letting it out. I think that bothers Marco. He usually can't talk about something that upsets him until he's had time to process it."

"You're an amazing mom, Gils. The twins are damn lucky to have you."

"Thanks, Nora. I hope they weren't too much trouble."

I rubbed my knee. Both of them, along with my elbow, had been getting sorer as the day passed. I shook my head. "They were no trouble at all."

Gilly snorted. "What happened?"

"Ari used my bathroom."

"Well, that's not so bad."

"While I was showering."

"That's worse."

"And she didn't announce herself until I came out of the shower."

"Oh boy."

"And then she screamed at me to put on a towel."

Gilly laughed. "That sounds like Ari."

"She acted like I was gross or something."

"To her teenage eyes, we both are."

"Other than a few bulges, some cellulite, and slightly baggy boobs, my body looks fantastic."

"I tell you that all the time, minus the checklist of your flaws." She chuckled, and it was great to see her smiling again. "You know, there is nothing more humbling to someone over the age of forty than a teenager. They tend to say the first thing that pops into their head, and they often have no idea when they've hurt someone's feelings. I wouldn't take it personally."

"I don't," I said. "I hadn't quite expected how invasive it would feel."

"They aren't parasites."

I raised a brow. "Are you sure about that?"

"Nora!"

I giggled. "I'm kidding. I love your kids. And I would do anything for them." I needed to make sure "anything" didn't include raising them while their mother rotted in prison.

I pulled down Rose Palace Road, the long drive leading to the resort. It, like most of the resorts in Garden Cove, had been built on a man-made cove that got its water supply from White River. The founders had named the town Garden Cove on account of all the wildflowers that grew rampant around the inlet.

Rose Palace, one of the founding resorts, had been built for grandeur, with tall white columns vaulting past the second floor. The foyer opened up to two grand staircases on either side, with guest relations centered between them on the first floor. The place was immaculately cleaned twice a day, and the resort employees wore white uniforms that looked freshly washed and pressed. Gilly had told me that all employees, regardless of their station at the Rose Palace, were required to change clothing if the white of their uniform was soiled while they were on shift. The owner believed people would pay for the fantasy of the perfect getaway, and he'd been right. It was the most expensive, but still the busiest, resort Garden Cove had.

"I'm going to go find Phil," Gilly said. "I'll be right back."

"Where is the security office?"

"Why?" she asked suspiciously.

"Because I'm going to poke around. Why do you think?"

"I think I need to keep my job, Nora. And that might be harder to do if my best friend gets caught ransacking Lloyd's office."

I crossed my heart. "No ransacking. I swear it. I'll take a casual look."

"To see if there is anything incriminating just lying around?"

She was being sarcastic, but it was exactly what I had planned. Of course, I was hoping that my new psychic senses would kick in as well. After my morning with Ezra, I had started to really hope that this gift had come along at this time in my life for a reason. To help my friend. "It could happen," I said.

"Fine." She pointed to double doors on the right.

"It's past those doors at the end of the corridor. The room is on the right. Lou Barrowman is probably working today. He's around our age, and he's fond of me, so..." She shrugged. "He might be willing to talk to you about Lloyd."

"Thanks for the tip."

Gilly strolled toward the reception desk, and I casually made my way to the double doors.

There was a sign on the door that stated, No Guests Beyond This Point.

Welp, good thing I wasn't a guest.

I pressed on the bar latch on the right door and felt a rush of exhilaration when it opened. It wasn't locked. Yay! I figured with it housing the security office that it might be, well, secure.

I glanced around to make sure no one was watching, then opened the door wide enough to scooch on in. When I was safely on the other side, I let out the breath I'd been holding. A jittery rush of adrenaline made my hands shake as I hastily made my way toward the security room. I worked up several stories in my head to tell this Lou guy if he was in the office and wanted to know why I was in an off-limits part of the resort.

None of them were necessary, however, because the room was empty. Lucky me.

I hit my sore elbow on the doorframe when I entered the office. There were black and white monitors set up on a desk against the wall, and it smelled of chemicals, ozone, and metal.

"We belong together." Lloyd latches onto both her wrists with his large hands. "You have to give me another chance."

"Get your hands off me," Gilly says, pain evident in her shaking voice.

"I'll never let you go." His voice is as menacing as I remember. "Never."

The door opens, a large, broad-shouldered man entering the room.

Lloyd lets go of Gilly. She rushes past the newcomer to flee the room. The new man has a bald head, and without a clear face, he reminds me of a djinn. "Mr. Williams wants to speak to you," he says.

There is a snarl of contempt in Lloyd's voice. "He could have called me."

"I'm just the messenger." The man doesn't leave right away. "Gilly looked upset. If you've hurt her, I swear—"

"Looks like someone has a crush," Lloyd snarls. "Stay away from her, Lou. Or I'll make you pay."

The bald man had to be Lou Barrowman. Gilly was right—he was fond of her. Enough to confront Lloyd.

I worked my way around the small room. There were invoices, a paper log for incidents, but since Lloyd hadn't been working that night, I'm not sure that was helpful. But the desk calendar? Now that was interesting. There were initials and numbers on different dates, and two days earlier, the day Lloyd died, there were the letters RL and the number 10 written down. Could that be Ricky Little? And Ezra had said there was probably ten thousand dollars in the package of cash.

A commotion on one of the monitors caught my

attention. The screens were small, so I put on my reading glasses for a closer look. Oops! Gilly was standing in front of a man in a dark suit. He looked angry, and she looked as if she were about to shove her own anger down his throat as she waved her hands and poked at the air.

A large bald man, most likely Lou, was patting the air beside Gilly in a "calm down" gesture.

Oh no. No. This was so flippin' bad. Gilly hated being told to calm down. Honestly, no woman enjoyed that oft-used patronizing statement. She was going to lose her mind.

There were other dates and letters on the calendar, so I took a quick photo with my phone then ran to the lobby like I had brand-new knees.

FIFTEEN

I escaped back through the double doors without detection, mostly because Gilly was better than an explosion when it came to diverting attention. All eyes were on her.

"I don't need to be escorted off the premises. Land-sakes, after all I've given to this place, you're going to fire me? What the hell, Phil?" she shouted at the man in the suit. "You can't fire me, because I fire *you*. You sorry son-of-a-bitch." She poked her finger in his direction. "I fire you!"

"Calm down, Gilly," the bald guy said again. "This isn't helping."

"I am calm," she seethed in a very un-calm manner. "When I'm not calm, you'll know it." Her eyes were even more bloodshot as tears streaked her face. I think my BFF had reached her limit of crappy news and even crappier men for one week.

"Gilly," I said. I put my hand on her shoulder. "Let's go."

"Gladly," she huffed. "This place sucks." She looked around at the gathered crowd of guests and employees. "The Rose Palace Resort does not give a flying fig about the welfare of its loyal employees," she said. "Think about that while you're eating your pillow mint tonight."

I tugged at her. "We should go now."

"Listen to your friend, Gilly. And good luck drawing unemployment, now that you've quit."

I'd had enough of this pompous ass. If I hadn't been worried about Gilly getting thrown back in jail, I would have let her at him.

Instead, I cut ties with a huge client of mine by pronouncing, "The Rose Palace has a bedbug infestation."

I watched with satisfaction as most of the resort guests who had circled us for the show headed toward the guest-relations counter. Then I looked at Phil Williams, and said, "You can take your unemployment and shove it up your—"

"Okay, Nora," Gilly said, smiling with pride. "I think I'm ready to go now."

As we headed out, she said, "You were awesome in there."

"What were you thinking?" I asked angrily. "What if your boss had called the cops? You could have ended up back in jail."

"I was thinking that without a job, that's where I'm going to end up, anyhow."

I shook my head. "You have a job," I told her. "You are now employee number two at Scents and Scentsability."

"You can't afford to pay me, Nora."

"Look, the shop used to be a diner. And it has a banquet room. I've been using it for storage, but there's no reason we can't convert it into a massage area. The room is large enough to be divided into two private spaces and seating for anyone waiting their turn."

"Seriously?" Gilly asked. "I wouldn't be able to pay you much to rent the space at first. That wouldn't be a fair trade-off."

"Until we get you out of this mess, I'm paying *you*," I said. "I will pay you a base salary, you keep all the money for the massages at first. And when your client load increases, we can adjust the base. You can encourage your clients to buy some of my products to offset the cost."

"That's too generous, Nora. I can't let you pay me."

"Since employment is a stipulation for your bail release, it's going to be mandatory."

Gilly was silent the rest of the way to my car. When we got back into town, I turned onto Gardenia Drive toward the Taco Shake Shack.

"I'll work for you, Nora. Gratefully, but I don't want you making any rash decisions about how to use the storage space."

"Did my plan sound like I'd made it up off the cuff?"

I asked. "Because this is something I've been thinking about for a long time. Your a-hole boss did me a huge favor by letting you go. I want you working with me at Scents and Scentsability. I mean, I don't know how many times I've tested the water with you. I didn't want to push too hard, because I know you had stability and health insurance with the Rose Palace." I turned into the Taco Shake Shack drive-through and got in line. When the car was idle, I glanced at Gilly apologetically. "I can't provide any insurance."

"Gio has the twins covered on his policy," she said. "It was part of the divorce decree."

"And he is still paying child support and alimony, right?"

She nodded.

"There you have it. We'll stop by the shop on the way home and get an I-9 employment form and a W-2 for you to fill out so we can drop it by the courthouse tomorrow."

"How'd I get so lucky?" Tears brimmed her eyes. "You are the bestest best friend."

I eased the car forward as the vehicles in front of me advanced. "I wish I could say this was all a magnanimous gesture out of the goodness of my heart, but honestly, Gilly. I couldn't have gotten through the last year and a half without you, and now that Mom's gone, I need you more than ever. This is completely selfish on my part. I. Need. You." Now, we were both crying.

"Welcome to the Taco Shake Shack," a voice over the speaker said as I pulled the car up to the menu. The system was the same one they'd been using for as long as I could remember, so it was hard to tell if the drive-through person was male or female. "What can I get you?"

"And now I need tacos," I said to Gilly. "Lots and lots of tacos." She snorted on a laugh, and a snotty bubble popped out of her nose. She wiped at it with the back of her sleeve. My own nose dripped from the ugly cry. Gilly's face was a blotchy wet mess.

"I didn't get your order," the voice said. "Can you repeat it?"

"I need two monster packs of your beef tacos, extra hot sauce, two large shakes, one chocolate and one pineapple banana." I sniffed and I looked around for a box of tissues. "And lots of extra napkins, please."

The drive through attendant read back the order. "And extra napkins," he or she added at the end.

"Lots of napkins," Gilly shouted across me to the speaker.

"That'll be fourteen dollars and eighty-nine cents at the window."

Gilly got out her wallet.

"Put that away. Lunch is on me," I said. I had forty dollars in cash in my wallet, and I knew that Gilly had spent her only cash to call us the night before from the jail. "These are your freedom tacos."

At the window, a young man with cystic acne poked his head out. "You had the monster packs and two large shakes."

"Chocolate and pineapple banana," I said.

He smiled. "Extra hot sauce and extra napkins."

"You got it." Gilly and I had to look frightening, but the young man didn't seem to notice. I'm sure he had customers who came through in worse condition than us. I know I'd gone through many a drive-through over the years in pajamas and my hair barely combed. Sometimes you just needed a Coke and fries, and that shouldn't have to include putting on a bra or makeup.

As we were leaving the Taco Shake Shack, the scent of greasy, awesome tacos filled my car. I slammed on my brakes when...

"This is the last time we'll get monster packs as high schoolers," a girl says. She is wearing a pair of tight, tight high-waisted jeans, a sweatshirt with the neck cut out, and her hair is mousy brown, permed and poofy. It takes me a minute to realize it's me. Holy, crap. It was the day before graduation.

Another girl, that I knew to be Gilly, wears her dark brown hair permed and poofy as well, along with her signature giant bangs. She crawls up on the picnic table. "We're finally free!" she squeals. She sings a line about pencils and books from Alice Cooper's "School's Out For Summer", ending with her favorite part where the school blows up. She is wearing black tights, an oversized blue sweater that hit her at the thighs, and hot pink leg warmers. To finish the look, Gilly, has on white high-top tennis shoes that match mine.

"Promise me we'll always be best friends," I say.

"Forever," she replies. I get up and walk around the corner to throw away a taco wrapper. Gilly uses a pen and scratches our initials into the picnic table.

"Nora!" I heard the alarm in Gilly's voice. Cars were honking behind us.

"I'm okay." I took my foot off the brake.

"No, you're not," she said. "Pull over, and I'll drive. Maybe we should call your doctor."

I parked and traded spots with Gilly, because having a vision while driving had scared me as much as my slamming on the brakes and zoning out had scared her. "I don't need the doctor."

"You passed out two nights ago, and you've been blanking a lot lately. Like you're in a daydream. The other night you were worried about a brain tumor. Now you have me worried you might actually have one."

"I'm having visions," I told her. "I can see the memories of other people when I smell a strong scent."

"Lots of people can recall memories," she said. "It doesn't usually require a hazard warning."

"Did you hear me? I can see *other* people's memories, Gilly."

"Here's the part where you yell *psych*!" She frowned at me. "You're serious. Okay. That's it. I really think we should call your doctor."

"I saw Lloyd grab you in the security office," I said.

"I told you about that."

"Yes, but I saw it before you told me. You were upset about what he'd said about Ari, and after you broke up with him, he grabbed you and told you he would never let you go. I wanted to kill him for you. The big bald guy —I assume it's Lou—came in and you escaped the room."

"I must have told you..."

"You didn't. I saw the Lou part today when I was back in that office. Scents trigger the visions."

"I want to believe you, Nora." Her brow creased and the lines along the side of her mouth deepened. "It's just so..."

"Impossible," I finished. "Yeah, that's what I thought. Weren't you just thinking about the last day of high school, when we came here for tacos?"

"Yes," she said. The disbelief crowding her face lessened. "But couldn't that have just been your memory? You were there, too. And we just got tacos."

"You wore your blue oversized sweater, the one with the shoulder pads, and me in my favorite jeans and sweatshirt. I made you promise that we would always be best friends."

She smiled. "You did. It's a promise we've always kept." She got us back on the road. "But that could still just be your memory."

"After you promised, I walked around the corner of the Taco Shake Shack to throw my trash away, and you scratched our initials into the picnic table. I never saw you do that in real life."

She turned onto a street to take us to her house.

"We need to get the paperwork from the shop."

"Later," she said. "Right now, we've got tacos and your new," she waved her hand, "whatever you are calling this scent-memory thingy."

I smiled. "Ezra called it Smell-O-Vision."

She tucked her chin. "It's Ezra now, huh?"

"It's not like that," I said. Although a part of me wished it was. "I had one of my psychic-ish episodes when I went to the Bar-B-Q Pit this morning, and he happened to catch me in the middle of it. I took a chance and told him about my scent ability. It's how we discovered the stack of cash in the dumpster."

"Wait. What?"

"Oh, right. I haven't told you about this, yet. I saw someone dragging Lloyd's body to the smoker." My hands became animated as I described the scene ending with the person throwing the money into the trash bin. "And then he put Lloyd's corpse into the meat smoker."

Gilly's lip curled. "Oh, how awful."

"He was already dead before he was placed in there," I reassured her. "Ezra—I mean, Detective Holden said Lloyd didn't have any smoke in his lungs."

"I wasn't worried about Lloyd. It's all that meat, the ribs, the briskets—oh merciful God, the brisket. All of it ruined. I hope when we find this killer, he rots in jail for life."

I liked how positive she sounded. "He will," I said. "I promise you, and you know I keep my word."

"So, what else have you seen?" Gilly asked. "Anything juicy?"

"You're as bad as Pippa." I rubbed my hands together. "Speaking of Pippa. Her and Jordy. Making out in the workroom."

"No!"

"Yes!" It was a rush telling her the news. "They are totally a couple."

"You know," Gilly said, "I had an inkling something was stirring with those two. Anything else?"

The redhead from my Lloyd memory. "Crap, there was one that I forgot to tell Ezra about. When Lloyd came to my house the other night, I saw a glimpse of him strangling a red-haired woman. She was pleading with him to stop, but he wouldn't. I think...I think he might have killed her."

"Christ, Nora. If that's true, I mean, what if he...that could have been me."

"But it wasn't," I said.

"Because someone killed him. I can't believe I let someone like that into my life." Her grip on the steering wheel turned her knuckles white. "You know, Lloyd was dating a woman with ginger-red hair the first year he was at the Rose Palace."

"What was her name?"

"It was Jessica or Jennifer, I think. Definitely a J-name. She would come in several times a week for a few months, then she stopped coming by. He said they broke up, but you don't think—" Her mouth gaped.

I nodded. "Maybe. Maybe she didn't just stop coming around. Maybe she tried to leave Lloyd like you did, and he made sure that she never got away."

SIXTEEN

"Wow, they did a number on my drawers," Gilly said. "I'm going to have to wash all my underwear. Although, I'm not sure I want to wear any of them after a bunch of strangers pawed through them."

I gave her a sneaky side-eye glance. "You've never minded strangers pawing your panties before."

She elbowed me in the ribs.

"Ow."

She smirked. "You deserved that one."

"I really did." I laughed.

"Well, at least they mostly left Ari and Marco's rooms alone." She sighed as she looked around her bedroom. The police search had left nearly everything in her house tossed, touched, and, in a few cases, taken. It's not like the cops had cleaned up before they'd left. I knew she had to feel violated and unsafe in her own home.

"Why don't you pack a bag? You and the twins can stay with me until this whole mess gets cleared up."

"Because your house is a two-bedroom, two-bath cottage home," Gilly said. "It's cozy for one but add another adult woman and two teenagers to the mix, and it becomes a nightmare on Jonquil Street."

"Clever." Still, I pouted. "It wasn't all bad having the kids there. I'm sure we could survive a couple of weeks together."

"I love you, Nora, but it's going to be a hard no." She laughed. "When is Detective Easy showing up?" She emptied her bras and underwear into a laundry basket.

I'd called Ezra after Gilly told me about Lloyd's disappearing girlfriend. It might not have been the same woman, but since Ezra was staying open-minded about my visions, I felt like I had to tell him. I hoped Jessica or Jennifer had gotten away from Lloyd, but what if she hadn't? What if she had family who was still looking for her now?

"He said he was on his way." I heard a car door shut and looked out Gilly's bedroom window. It was Mr. Garner. He had Godiva with him, and she danced around him as he carried a bag into his house.

"Not Detective Hottie?" Gilly asked.

"How'd you know?"

"I don't have to be psychic to know when you're disappointed, Nora."

"Oh." I made a face. "That obvious, huh?"

"Only to me." She put her arms around my shoulders. "You really like him, huh?"

"I think I do. He's younger than me, though."

"By how much?"

"Eleventy-billion years."

"Right. More like he's in his thirties. So, probably fifteen years or less younger than you. If the roles were reversed, no one would think twice."

"So that makes me a cougar. A cradle robber."

"A WILF," she said.

"What's a WILF?"

"Woman I'd Liked to F—"

"Shut up," I said, batting her shoulder. I followed her as she carried the basket down the hall to the laundry room. "Besides, I don't have anything to offer a man that young."

"You have the same thing to offer that someone his age would have to offer, Nora. You're fifty-one, not ninety-one."

"You're right. But I haven't liked someone this much since Shawn. You know the feeling you get when you want the guy so much it makes you scared to act because you're worried you'll say something or do something to completely screw it up?"

"You felt that way with Shawn?"

I nodded. "All the time when we first started going out. It eventually went away, but the fear was real. I feel that same kind of anxiety about Ezra."

"I know what you need to do," Gilly said.

"Run away?" I asked.

"No, jump his bones. Get him out of your system."

I laughed. "I don't even know if my vagina still works."

Gilly grunted her surprise. "You mean you haven't..." She held up two fingers.

"Nope, I've never joined the Boy Scouts," I said.

"You know what I mean."

I did. "I've only been cleared to resume stuff down there since Friday." Before that, my doctor had forbidden it. Just like straining to poop, orgasms could tear internal sutures as well. It was hard talking about my fears about my own body, even with Gilly. "I've read that some women may not be able to achieve orgasms afterward. It's rare but it happens. You know I joined a few online hysterectomy groups. I can't tell you how many women talked about vaginal dryness. It was already dusty down there from two years of no whoopie. Gilly, vaginal dryness is not sexy!"

"There's this newfangled stuff they sell at the store these days," she said in her best Katherine Hepburn impression. "It's called lube, and it slicks the slit, lickety-split."

I almost choked on my laugh.

Gilly laughed, too, then added, "I like Astroglide the best. Get it. I've been going through peri-menopause for the past two years, and it's like I have the va-jay-jay of a twenty-year-old every time."

I mentally made a note to buy Astroglide the next time I went to the pharmacy.

A knock at the front door made my heart skip a beat. "I'll go get it," I said.

Gilly gave me a pat on the booty, and said, "Go get him, Tiger."

In my case it was more like cougar, but whatever. I tried to hide my disappointment when I opened the front door to find Mr. Garner holding an empty casserole dish.

"Hi," I greeted him. "Do you want to talk to Gilly?"

"I wanted to return her dish." He held it out to me. "It was a lovely roast. Will you tell her I said so?"

"I will." Mr. Garner was such a sweet man. "I'm really sorry about your wife. Gilly told me this time of year is hard for you."

His eyes closed for a moment. "It was hard losing her."

"Was she from around here? Gilly says you and she used to vacation here at Garden Cove."

"She wasn't. We were both city slickers, but we had bought a cabin on the cove to spend a month here every summer after I retired."

"What line of work were you in?"

"I was in the Army for twenty-eight years. Retired as a master sergeant with an infantry group out of Fort Leonard Wood."

"Thank you for your service," I said.

He shuffled his feet then nodded. "Don't forget to tell Gilly what I said about the roast," he said.

A red truck came down the lane. My palms sweat as Ezra parked out on the street. Mr. Garner's gaze followed mine.

"I can't let this go on," he said. "I have to tell you—"

Ezra came up behind him. "Hello," he said. He gave Mr. Garner a cordial smile. "If you'll excuse us, Mr. Garner. I have some police business I have to discuss with Ms. Black and Ms. Martin."

The old man moved out of Ezra's way. "Can I just say—"

"I'm really sorry," I told him. "I'll give the dish to Gilly and tell her that you liked the meal she sent you."

"I need you to—"

I wasn't trying to be rude to the man, but I really wanted to see if Ezra had found anything about the J-named woman from my vision. "Another time, okay?"

"No!" Mr. Garner shouted. "Not another time. Now. This has to happen now." His voice held the command of a leader.

Gilly jogged up the hallway. "What is going on out here?"

"I, uhm, think Mr. Garner wants to tell us something," I said.

"What is it, sir?" Ezra asked. "Do you have new information about the case?"

The old man's chin trembled. "I need to show you. You won't understand unless you see for yourself," he said. "Will you come to my house?"

Ezra nodded. "We can go right now."

The three of us, Gilly, Ezra, and me, followed Mr. Garner across the lawn to his home. His was a ranch house, something I envied. If I had thought about the difficulty of getting up and down stairs all the time, I probably would have bought a ranch house as well.

Godiva barked her little fuzzy head off until Mr. Garner opened the door and we followed him inside.

The house was neatly kept, with sparse furnishings, but he'd moved here alone and his house reflected his bachelorhood. There was one recliner in the living room with a forty-inch flat-screen television mounted on the wall over a faux fireplace. The kitchen had a four-chair round table, and basic appliances like a toaster, microwave, stove and refrigerator. He had an open package of Double Stuf Oreos and an empty milk glass sitting on the counter.

"What did you want to show us, Mr. Garner?" I asked.

"It's just down the hall," he said. He stopped in front of the second door on the right. "In here."

I could smell vanilla and cinnamon along with burned wax emanating from the room. Scented candles most likely. The old gentleman was acting mysteriously, and I couldn't help but feel a sense of trepidation as we waited.

Mr. Garner finally opened the door and gestured for us to enter first. He followed with Godiva on his heels.

The walls were like something out of a thriller movie. Mr. Garner had pictures all over the place of a young woman with red hair. Dozens of photographs of her alone and several of her with friends. In one picture, Mr. Garner had his arm around her shoulders. He and the woman were smiling. Right below that picture was another one with the woman and a younger Lloyd Briscoll.

I dropped down into a squat, suddenly overwhelmed by the scent of cinnamon to the point that it made my head spin and my stomach burn.

"Gilly! Get out here!" I can't see his face, as usual, but I know it's Lloyd by his voice. "You can't threaten me and get away with it. You want to end someone, well, come and get me, you stupid bitch, I'm right here. You know what? I'll end you! I'll choke the life outta you!"

I can see him from inside a window, but I'm not in Gilly's house. It's a man in the window. The hair and body mark him as Gilly's neighbor. Mr. Garner watches Lloyd as he rants and raves in Gilly's driveway. Apparently, he'd gotten out of jail and had driven right to Gilly's house. She wasn't home yet because the house was completely dark.

Mr. Garner goes into the kitchen, opens a drawer, and pulls out a knife.

He goes outside and crosses Gilly's lawn.

"Go home, Lloyd," he says. "Leave Gilly alone now."

"Shut your gobhole," Lloyd shouts. He stumbles toward Mr. Garner, his fists raised. "Or I'll shut it for you."

Mr. Garner keeps the knife belly level. "I'll call the police if you don't leave."

"And then what? They won't do a thing to me, you old bastard. I am untouchable."

"No one's untouchable, young man." Mr. Garner's hand is remarkably steady. "I don't understand how my Maxine ever dated you."

Lloyd barks out a laugh. He comes close to Mr. Garner, much the way he had when he pressed himself against the barrel of my gun. God, the man was arrogant. Not to mention stupid. *"If you don't get back in your house, old man, I'll kill you. Then I'll reunite you with your darling daughter."*

Mr. Garner jabs the knife into Lloyd's stomach. Lloyd staggers back. "Where is she?" yells Mr. Garner. "Where is Maxine?"

I opened my eyes.

Well, damn. I was on the floor again. Ezra and Gilly knelt on either side of me. Mr. Garner stood near the doorway, his expression worried. Godiva sat at my feet. She butted my leg, and I automatically stroked her head. I don't know if I was comforting her or myself. Either way, the feel of her soft fur under my fingertips helped settle me.

Tears leaked from my eyes as I met Mr. Garner's gaze. "I'm sorry," I said, my voice hoarse. "I'm sorry Lloyd killed Maxine. But..." I trailed off, unable to condemn the man who'd suffered so much death and sorrow.

"I shouldn't have stabbed him," Mr. Garner finished for me. "I know. But I'm not sorry he's dead. I'll never be sorry that murdering bastard got what he deserved."

SEVENTEEN

"I should've come forward sooner," Mr. Garner said. He looked at Godiva, who'd taken up a spot between my legs. She stared up at him, not moving. Her liquid brown eyes looked so sad.

Ezra helped me up to sit in the office chair in front of a computer desk, the only furniture, other than a file cabinet, in the room. Godiva stretched up, putting her paws on my calf. I picked her up and put her in my lap. I don't know why the dog was all about me—but I was happy to hold her.

"How in the world did you have my knife?" Gilly asked.

"The knife was with the roast you sent over a couple of months ago. I meant to return it, but it was such a good blade, and then you never asked for it back."

Ah, the roast. He'd returned the dish after Gilly got home today because he'd been trying to work up the courage to tell the truth.

My BFF swallowed hard, obviously upset. And probably trying to come to terms with the idea her nice elderly neighbor had killed Lloyd. "Why try to frame me?"

"I wasn't thinking straight," Mr. Garner said. "I grabbed the sharpest knife out of my drawer—yours. I never intended to actually stab him." He looked down at his hands. Even though he'd professed he wasn't sorry about killing Lloyd, I couldn't help but think he was imagining blood on his hands.

He gestured to the pictures. "Maxine told me she was dating a police officer. I thought she'd be safe with a cop. He could protect her, right? Then she disappeared." Rage twisted his features. He crossed the room and tore the picture of Lloyd and Maxine off the wall. "Ten years! That's how long it's been since I've seen my daughter. And my wife...she couldn't deal with our only child's loss. She died of a broken heart." He stared at the photo. "I mean that literally. Broken heart syndrome. So, I lost her, too."

He ripped the picture into tiny pieces and let them drift like snowflakes onto the floor. "Lloyd helped me look for Maxine, you know. He came to my wife's funeral. I thought he'd gotten railroaded when he was fired from the police force. Then...then I saw him at the Bar-B-Q Pit. How he treated Gilly. How he threatened and bullied everyone."

"You realized Lloyd wasn't a good man," said Ezra gently. I saw that he'd put his hand on his gun hip. "And that he could've hurt Maxine."

"He admitted it," said Mr. Garner. "Told me he'd kill me and reunite me with my little girl."

I felt for the old guy, I really did. But I wasn't magnanimous enough to forgive him for putting Gilly through hell.

But Gilly, with her marshmallow heart, put her hand on Mr. Garner's shoulder and squeezed. "People like Lloyd are good at showing you exactly what you want to see. That's their fault. Not yours." She had used my words to her in an act of true forgiveness. She proved, once again, why she was the heart of our dynamic duo.

Ezra cleared his throat. "I'm going to have to arrest you and take you downtown, Mr. Garner."

The old man nodded. "I expect so." His gaze settled on me and Godiva as the old man put his arms behind his back and allowed Ezra to cuff him. "Looks like she's picked you," he said. "You mind looking out for her until..." He shook his head. "I don't know. Might be a long time before I see her again."

"I'll take her," I said, my throat knotted. I didn't have a great track record with kids, plants, or animals, but Godiva had parked herself in my lap. I couldn't *not* take her. "But first...why did you drive Lloyd all the way to the Bar-B-Q Pit and put him in the smoker? And why burn down the restaurant? And why throw ten grand away in the dumpster?"

Ezra stared hard at me, but I ignored him. I knew he'd interrogate Mr. Garner at the station where I couldn't ask questions or hear the answers, but damn it, I wanted to know.

169

Mr. Garner's arms went slack, and his eyes widened. "I... In the smoker. What?"

"Lloyd was found in the smoker at the back of the Pit," I said.

"Nora." Ezra's brows dipped. "That's enough."

"Now, wait a minute," sputtered Mr. Garner. "I didn't take Lloyd anywhere. I didn't burn down the restaurant. And I don't know anything about the money."

"Please, stop talking Mr. Garner." Ezra Mirandized the old man, then added, "I suggest you take the 'remain silent' part seriously."

"Look, Detective Holden, I only stabbed Lloyd in the stomach. He got in his car and took off. I went back into my house."

I shared a look with Ezra. I knew Lloyd had died with the knife in his *chest*, not his stomach.

Mr. Garner looked over his shoulder at Ezra. "I confessed to killing him, okay? But I didn't dump his body or burn down the Pit or throw away money. And... and *I* stabbed him with Gilly's knife, so that's enough to get Gilly out of trouble, right?"

Ezra sighed. "The knife was wiped clean. No prints. Right now, a case could be made for the two of you working together."

Gilly's mouth dropped open, and so did mine. I glared at him. *"What?"*

"Gilly and Mr. Garner are next-door neighbors. Gilly still doesn't have an alibi. Two people could more easily put the body in the smoker—and set the Pit on fire."

Mr. Garner looked crushed. "I've made this whole situation worse."

"No," I said. "This whole situation sucks." I picked up Godiva and put her on the floor, much to her disliking. "There was no reason to burn down the Pit if Lloyd was in the smoker. And why would anyone throw away ten thousand dollars?"

"I don't know," Ezra admitted. "Come on, Mr. Garner. I'll take you to booking."

GODIVA WAS on my heels as I paced in Gilly's living room. "Can you believe this? Mr. Garner confesses and Ezra still wants you to go to the pokey for the crime."

"He doesn't want me to go to jail. He is thinking like an investigator, Nora. He has to consider all the angles."

"Stop defending him." I waved my hands, agitation making my skin vibrate. "We have to do something. We have to figure out why the Pit was burned down and why the real killer threw away a brick of cash."

"Well, obviously whoever it was wanted to retrieve it later."

"But why not just take it with him—or her?"

"Because he—or she—couldn't?"

I tried to work it out in my head. Mr. Garner stabs Lloyd. Lloyd staggers to his car and...doesn't go to the hospital? Okay. Maybe he calls someone for help. And that someone meets him at the Pit, which makes no sense, and then...removes the knife and stabs Lloyd in the chest?

Argh!

"Let's say Lloyd calls someone for help. But they see an opportunity. Lloyd was an asshat; it's not a stretch to say he had a few enemies."

"Frenemies, too," added Gilly. She sat on the couch, watching me wear a path in her carpet. Godiva got tired of following me and lay down near the coffee table, her brown eyes glued to me.

"Okay," I said. "Frenemy. Why go to the Pit?"

"Arson? Still River burned down, too."

"Do you think Lloyd was paid ten grand to burn down the Pit?"

"And maybe he got paid to set fire to Still River, too? But why would he do that?" Gilly frowned. "Who'd want to burn down the restaurants in Garden Cove?"

"Good questions. So. Killer can't take the money with them. Whatever the reason. Tosses the cash in the dumpster with the intention of coming back for it later."

"So Lloyd was stabbed for the money?"

"I think Ezra was right about two killers," I said. "Well, one attempted murder and the other one finished it. Mr. Garner stabs him. Lloyd takes off and calls someone for help. The real murderer—who stabs him again, this time really killing Lloyd. But why are they at the Pit? Why would Lloyd go there and not an emergency room?"

Gilly shook her head. "This is why we're not investigators, Nora."

My cellphone vibrated in my pants pocket. I withdrew it and looked at the display. I made a face. "Ezra."

"Talk to him."

I answered the call.

"I know you're upset with me," said Ezra right after I said a gruff hello. "But I'd like to ask for your help. Lloyd lived in a small farmhouse on eight acres outside of town. I was thinking you could use your super sniffer to help us search his place."

"For more evidence against Gilly?" I asked. "I don't think so."

"I'm inclined to believe she's innocent," said Ezra. "But right now, even with Mr. Garner's confession, she's not off the hook. There's another reason, too. Maybe Maxine is buried out there. And with your nose for trouble..."

"A scent might trigger a vision."

"Exactly," said Ezra. "But there's one catch."

"Figures. What?"

"You gotta convince Chief Rafferty to let you snoop around."

CHAPTER
EIGHTEEN

"How in the world can I convince Shawn about my weird power?" I asked. Shawn still thought of me as the person I had been decades ago, and I sure as heck didn't have a supernatural sniffer then. "He won't believe me."

"Show him what you can do. Whether it's regular human intuition or a paranormal ability, you wouldn't be the first psychic to help the police track a murderer."

"Have you met my ex-husband?" I scoffed.

"You're a persuasive woman," he said. "If you put your mind to it, I have no doubt you'll convince the chief that you can help."

I definitely wanted to help find evidence that would get Gilly out of this mess. And what if I could help bring closure to Mr. Garner? He might've made some bad decisions, but the man had suffered greatly. "Okay," I finally said.

"That's my girl."

"Not yet," I said, butterflies fluttering in my stomach. "But maybe I could be."

"Good to know," he said, his voice low and sultry. Then he added, "Meet me at the station in half an hour. You and I can go talk to the chief. That sound all right?"

"I'll be there."

———

EZRA and I waited outside Shawn's office. Anxiety twisted through me until I felt like I couldn't breathe. Shawn and I hadn't exactly left things on the best of terms, and I knew full well he'd sooner believe pigs could fly than I had scent-induced visions." With my knuckle, I rapped Ezra's knee. "I take it back. I don't want to do this."

"The chief won't bite," Ezra said. "Or maybe he will, you'd probably know better than I would."

"I haven't known what Shawn Rafferty would do in over twenty years," I said.

Ezra chuckled.

"What?"

"Twenty years ago, I was in middle school."

"How old are you?" I asked.

"It's not polite to ask a man his age," Ezra teased.

"I knew it. You're a baby."

"I'm thirty-two, but I haven't been a baby since I was sixteen. Getting your high school sweetheart pregnant during your junior year forces you to grow up."

"Sixteen, sweet Jeezus. I can't even imagine."

"I thought we had it all figured out, as you do at that age. We even convinced our folks to let us get married. Well, I convinced my dad. I lived with Kati and her parents until our high school graduation. She started college, and I worked sixty hours a week doing factory work." Ezra looked tired when he said it. "Her parents helped take care of Mason, but our relationship fell apart pretty fast after that. Married at sixteen, divorced at nineteen."

"And you never remarried?"

"Nope," he said. "I joined the police academy as soon as I turned twenty-one. Was hired on as a patrol officer in Springfield, then started taking criminal justice classes online and completed my degree in a few years. I never really had time for a wife."

"What about your son?"

"I've always tried to make time for Mason, but probably not enough. Doing the family counseling sessions with him and Kati really opened my eyes to how much he needed me."

Ezra was refreshingly forthcoming about his life. Even the parts that might not be so flattering.

"What about you?" he asked. "No burning interest in remarrying? Or having kids?"

"Nope."

Shawn stood in the doorway, his expression puzzled. "Nora never wanted a family."

Damn it. I'd been so wrapped up in my conversation with Ezra, I hadn't heard Shawn open the door.

"That's not true, Shawn. I wanted a family. I just

didn't want children." I got up and strolled past him. "You told me you wanted the same things. You changed. Not me. Why are you rehashing this?" I said. I wasn't angry with him, not really. But I couldn't understand why my life now was any of his business or why he was letting it affect him. "You got the life you wanted. And I'm happy for you, Shawn."

"I'm sorry, Nora." Shawn shook his head. "You didn't deserve that from me."

I nodded. "I know."

He glanced at Ezra. "Are you coming in, Detective Holden?" Shawn asked. "Or are you going to hang out in the hallway all day?"

"I'm coming in, sir."

"YOU WANT NORA TO DO WHAT?" Shawn's eyes practically bulged out of his head, and I hoped Ezra still had a job after today.

"It was my idea, Shawn," I said quickly. I had no problem telling a lie to keep Ezra out of trouble. To be honest, I probably would've come up with the same idea given enough time. He just got there before I did.

"You're not a psychic, Nora. And even if you were, I have never and would never hire a psychic to assist on a case." I was betting he was thanking his lucky stars that he'd divorced me now. He laughed, the sound full of disbelief. "Did you actually think I would go for this?"

"She can prove it," Ezra said.

I drew a finger across my throat as a warning to stop. Shawn might not be able to divorce me twice, but he could sure fire Ezra once.

Shawn tipped his head to the side. "Fine," he said. "Nora, if you can prove you're a psychic, I'll not only let you go out to Briscoll's home and dig around with your hoodoo nonsense, I'll send a team with you to help."

"Okay," I said. I let out a slow breath. "That sounds fair."

"Wait." Shawn raised his hand. "There's more. If you fail to convince me of your almighty powers, then you will stay out of this investigation and any *future* investigations. I really don't want to throw you in jail, Nora, but I will."

Talk about performance anxiety. I wasn't sure if I could keep my end of the deal if he couldn't be convinced. Until Gilly was in the clear, I wasn't about to stop getting her justice. Still, I nodded my agreement. "All right, then. I need something with a scent or strong odor."

"I can take off my shoes," Shawn said.

"Eww, no, Shawn." I shook my head. "Please don't."

He chuckled. He gestured around his office. "This room holds a lot of memories for me, so you see if you can find one. I'm sure something will have an odor."

He obviously found this whole scenario amusing, but it reminded me that Shawn had always been less than supportive when it came to beliefs that didn't match his own. "Show me the evidence," he would say. "Can you cite your sources?" Questions like those had sometimes made me feel more like a suspect than his wife.

Huh. It may have taken twenty-some years, but I realized that there was maybe more wrong with our relationship than our ideas about the components of a family.

As I made my way around Shawn's office, I picked up two awards, a picture of him with the governor, an air plant, a clay pinch pot that had *Jacob, 6 years old* scratched into the bottom. And I sniffed each and every one of them, feeling more and more foolish. "Come on Smell-O-Vision. Don't fail me now."

"You got this, Nora," Ezra said. "Just relax."

I gave him a tight-lipped smile. I appreciated the encouragement, but on the other hand, if I couldn't make some magic happen here, I'd lose the chance to help my best friend.

The other day I'd gotten a vision from smelling Shawn's cologne. In desperation, I strolled around to his side of the desk, stooped down so that my nose was at his neck, and I inhaled deep.

He leaned away from me, looking alarmed. "What are you doing?"

A woman sits under a bay window, she is wearing a floral head scarf as she sips her tea. The sun casts rays across the floor. A gray cat walks over into the path of warmth, stretches, and then flops over onto its back.

I see the man dressed in a dark blue suit with thin lapels. He wraps his arms around the woman. "How are you feeling today?" It's Shawn's voice.

She cups his face with her palms. "I'm all right, dear. The medicine the doctor gave me for the nausea is working." She leans back and turns her face into his neck. Even though her face is a blur, I can hear her inhale his scent. I smell it, too. Woodsy, earthy. "This is my happy place," she says.

"You're going to beat this," he tells her.

"It's cancer, not a sport." She says it softly, not maliciously.

"I have to go to work." He kisses her.

Only when he's gone, does she slide the scarf off her bald head and cry.

Shawn rolled his chair away from me as he got to his feet. "What in the world, Nora? Boundaries."

"I'm sorry, Shawn." I fought my own tears.

"For what?"

"Leila. She's lost all her hair now."

"How could you possibly—" He shook his head. "No. There is nothing in this room that reminds me of her...illness."

"It wasn't your memory, Shawn," I said gently. "It was hers. She has a strong emotional connection to your cologne. Prism Specter, right?"

"It's her favorite," he said. "I wear it for her so she can..." His tone was hollow. I saw the moment his disbelief melted away and desperation took its place. "Will she make it?"

"I only see memories, Shawn," I said. "But I can tell you that she's acting strong for you."

He nodded slowly and still appeared pained. "I'm not sure if I'm completely convinced, but a deal's a deal.

Holden, get a team together and head out to Briscoll's place."

———

LLOYD'S FARMHOUSE had been his childhood home. When his parents retired, Lloyd bought the house and property from them, and they used that money to move to Texas. The house was small and tidy, but not freakishly clean. The furniture looked dated, and I figured he'd left the house the way his parents kept it. Ezra had enlisted the help of Reese McKay, her partner, Carl Grigsby, and two other officers, Bill Thompson and Jeanna Treece.

Ezra had asked the others to wait outside while we looked over the inside of the house. I was grateful. It seemed the more intense the vision, the bigger the toll it took on my body. Besides, I felt more comfortable without the audience.

Ezra sifted through some cupboards in the kitchen. "Anything?" he asked.

"Not yet." That was the third time he'd asked. I hoped this wasn't going to turn into a cop version of *Are we there, yet?*

"You look cute in your glasses," he said.

"Focus," I replied.

"I am focused."

"No, I mean I need them to focus."

He grinned and shook his head. With my reading glasses on, up-close objects were nice and clear, but the distant items reminded me of the hazy faces in my visions. I wondered if those were out of focus because my eyes were old or if that was just how the memories worked. Whatever the case was, I hoped it would kick in soon. Lloyd's house had the musty scent of disuse. While it wasn't triggering psychic events, it was making my nose itch.

"I'm not getting anything in the kitchen. I'll go to the living room next." The last places I wanted to sniff around were the bathroom and the bedrooms. I might end up with some memories that would take getting a lobotomy to forget. After all, Gilly had dated and presumably slept with the guy, and if there was even a hint of a memory of her in his house, I did not want to see it.

The living room had a love seat and matching chair with an ottoman, along with a rocking chair that sat in the corner near the fireplace. I took a big whiff of a quilt and got a memory of his mom bringing his dad a beer. Not the earth-shattering evidence I was hoping for.

I walked over to the fireplace and sat down in the rocking chair. The scent of wood and soot caught my olfactory attention. I bent over to take in more of the smell.

A man stands in front of the burning wood in the fire-place. He stokes the flames with a poker then replaces it in the stand. After a few seconds of rubbing his hands together to warm them up, he reaches for the shelf, a wood slab the width of the hearth and just above the insert. He carefully lifts it off the hooks it is attached to and removes it. Behind the shelf is a hole in the brick mantel. He takes a key from his pocket and places it in the slot then returns the shelf to its proper place.

"Ezra!" I shouted when the vision ended.

He legged it into the living room. "You see something?"

I started pulling the knickknacks off the mantel. "Help me," I said. "It's behind here."

"What's behind here?" He grabbed the shelf when I finished clearing it.

"The key," I said.

"The key to what?"

"That's the question. It's important enough to hide, though, so I think it's important enough for us to find out."

NINETEEN

Ezra struggled to unlatch the shelf from its hooks, but after a few failed attempts, he succeeded. I bounced and gave a little *squeee* of joy. The hole in the brick was where I'd seen it, but would the key still be there?

"Success!" I shouted when Ezra tugged out an old-fashioned metal key. "What do you think it goes to?"

He examined it, turning the long key in his hand. "It's made of iron, you can tell from all the oxidation."

"Okay, Bill Nye, in these parts they call that rust."

Ezra rolled his eyes. "This looks like one of the keys that are used on a steamer trunk."

"That seems a weird piece of info to know."

"My mom had one." He went to the front door. "All right," he called out. "Come on in."

The four officers entered the house and waited for instructions.

Ezra held up the key. "We are looking for a trunk, a

box, or a door with a lock on it. I want this place searched from top to bottom. And if that doesn't get us anywhere, we'll tear up the floorboards. Somewhere in this house is a mystery container, and we are going to unlock it. Now, everyone split up and take a room. Don't move on until you've exhausted all the possibilities. If you find a hole that might fit this key, holler at me, and I'll come give it a try."

The cops nodded and dispersed. McKay took the upstairs, Grigsby the basement, Thompson and Treece took the bedrooms—ugh—and Ezra took the bathrooms. That left me with the living room and kitchen, and since we'd covered those two rooms thoroughly, it left me with some time to step outside and get some fresh air.

The vibrant hues of tangerine and blood orange highlighted the clouds covering the setting sun. It was absolutely stunning. I walked back toward the side of the house to stretch my legs and to look around, since I was useless inside. Out back of Lloyd's place, probably a hundred feet from the home, was a shed-like structure. A well house, maybe? It seemed awfully far away from the house to store tools or a lawn mower.

I stepped around a decorative windmill that was about two decades past decorative and headed over. When I got there, I could hear a whirring click inside. The door was metal. I reached out to test if it was locked. It was. Much to my disappointment, the lock was a modern bolt, so the key we found wouldn't fit it.

"What did you find?" a woman asked.

I whipped around, startled that I hadn't heard her coming. "Oh, hi, Officer McKay."

She smiled. "Call me Reese."

"Okay, Reese." I looked back toward the house. The lighting inside was dim because of the curtains, and I suddenly felt farther away from safety than I liked. "Didn't find anything upstairs, huh?"

"Nothing, so far," she said. "This looks interesting though. What do you think is in there?"

"It's locked."

McKay approached the door. She gave the handle a rattle. "It is," she said. "We could probably pop the door off its hinges. We'd need a crowbar, but it's doable."

"Okay. That sounds like a plan. This place doesn't have a garage. Where would Lloyd have kept his tools?"

"I'm not sure, but I have some in the trunk of my car."

"Cool. I'll wait here for you."

She nodded. "Is it true you can see psychic memories? Even from the dead?"

"What?"

"Word gets around," she said. "I overheard the chief talking to Ezra. So, can you?"

I shrugged. "It seems so, but I'm not sure how or why it works like that."

"Hmm," she said. "I'll be right back with a crowbar."

"I'll be waiting." She left, and I started getting the heebie-jeebies. "Maybe I won't wait," I muttered as I started back for the house. Thompson and Grigsby were on the front porch. I waved at them. "There's a well shed behind the house. The door is locked. Reese went to go get a crowbar."

Ezra and Treece came out of the house.

Ezra shook his head. "Can't find anything inside."

"Maybe it's because it's outside." Like in the well house.

Reese showed up with a crowbar in hand. "Who wants to hold the flashlight?"

"Not it," I said. My legs felt like they were made of lead. "I'm going to stay here. You guys can give me the crib notes when you get it open." They left as a unit, which seemed like overkill, but you couldn't blame them for wanting to know what was behind the locked door. It was human nature to be curious.

I forced my legs to move up the steps. The rails helped, but damn I was exhausted. The house might make my nose itchy, but the rocking chair was calling for me. I went inside and collapsed into the seat. The *errr-eeee err-eeee* noise the chair made was soothing, and I did not resist the urge to close my eyes. *Errr-eeee errr-eeee* repeated like a lullaby.

The more relaxed I felt, the stronger the smoke and soot aroma grew.

"I can't do this anymore, Lloyd. I won't. I'm tired of being blackmailed by you."

"Then you shouldn't have taken money from Phil Williams," Lloyd says. *"Once you're on his payroll, you're on there for good."*

"That was years ago," the man says.

"Once is all it takes. Phil records everything." Lloyd paces

187

the floor in front of his fireplace. "Look. It's three jobs. Ten-thousand dollars a score. And no one gets hurt. It's win-win."

"There is nothing win-win about burning down businesses so Phil can buy the properties cheap."

"You can help me for ten grand or you can help me for free, but you will help me." Lloyd moves the rocking chair aside, lifts the board directly underneath it, and pulls up a lockbox. It's a combination lock, 1, 2, 2, 4, and he opens the lid. Inside is several bricks of cash, like the one in the dumpster. He takes a bundle out. "Here," he says to the man, "Take it. You can be dirty and rich or dirty and broke. Either way, you're dirty."

The man reaches for the bundle.

I opened my eyes, bracing my knees to stop the rocking. Damn. Lloyd had been responsible for the arson at Still River. He'd been dead before the fire at the Bar-B-Q Pit. But it didn't matter, because even without a face in my vision, I now knew the identity of his accomplice.

I got up and moved the rocking chair a few feet back and tugged up the board. Inside was the lockbox I'd seen in the vision. My heart raced, and it was hard to catch my breath as I pulled the metal box from its hidey-hole.

I heard footsteps on the front porch.

"Ezra!" I shouted. "I found it!"

Instead of Ezra, Carl Grigsby strolled inside the house. "Detective Holden and the others are still trying to open the door back there. He sent me in to check on you."

"I'm fine," I said. I moved toward the front door, the box in front of me and the wall to my back.

"Are you okay, Nora? Holden says you get dizzy sometimes after one of your...episodes."

"Nope. I'm dandy. A-okay."

"So, it's true. You can see private, personal memories that don't belong to you."

My mouth was dry. "You know, it's not science. Besides, I could just be bonkers."

"Yeah? Then how did you know where Lloyd kept his dirty money?"

I swallowed hard. Of all the people to return to the house, why did it have to be Lloyd's accomplice and probable killer? I kept easing my way toward the door until my leg bumped the wrought-iron fireplace tool set. It clanged against the floor as it fell.

"I can't let you go, Ms. Black," he said. "I'm sorry. I didn't want this. I didn't want any of it."

"But you took the cash." I had to keep him talking. A talking bad guy was one who wasn't trying to kill you. "You had to know that things could go wrong. But why kill Lloyd?"

"Opportunity. The fool called me to help him. He'd been stabbed in the stomach, but still wanted to burn down the Pit." Carl's voice was eerily calm. "He even tried to pay me again."

He had his hand on his gun holster. I knew it was spring-loaded, and he could draw on me faster than I could run, so I kept talking. I don't know how he would explain shooting me, but Grigsby probably had a good story at the ready. "Is that why you threw the money in the dumpster? I thought you were hiding it, but you weren't, were you? You were literally throwing it away."

"I hoped Rita and Nancy would find it," he said. He seemed pleased with himself for the gesture, so I played along.

"That was considerate of you," I said. Inside, I was screaming, *you burned their flippin' business down and ruined the best smoker around, you idiot.* But it didn't seem wise to give voice to my complaint. Given the weird gleam in his eyes, I was beginning to think Grigsby was one taco short of a Taco Shake Shack combo platter.

Grigsby nodded. "Now Phil won't leave me alone. He wants me to pick up where Lloyd left off. Give me the box, Nora. Give it to me so I can use the money to make a new life somewhere else."

"Okay, but one question first. Do you know what Lloyd did with Maxine Garner's body?"

Grigsby blinked. "Maxine Garner? That missing girl from ten years ago?"

"She wasn't missing," I said. "Lloyd killed her."

His hand moved off his gun for a moment. "I..." He rubbed his face with his free hand. "Christ, what have I gotten myself into?"

"It's not too late to give yourself up. You can't get away."

"With that box, I can," he said. He pulled his weapon and pointed it at me. "I don't want to hurt you, Nora, so don't make me ask you again."

Dad hadn't raised a fool. He'd taught me that in situations like these, always assume your attacker will kill you, even if he says he won't. And I didn't believe for one minute that Grigsby was going to let me live. He'd already said as much. I think the only thing stopping him was that he wanted my death quick and quiet so he could escape before the other cops found me.

Just what the hell was in the well house that was taking up so much of their attention? "Okay," I said. "I'm going to give you the box. I'll set it down in front of me and kick it over to you. Is that all right?"

Grigsby nodded. "But no funny business."

"None," I agreed. I bent at the knees and they creaked like rusty hinges. Grigsby heard them because he made a face. "I fell in the shower this morning," I said.

"You should probably see a doctor," he replied as if he didn't plan to kill me. He gestured with his free hand. "Get on with it already."

I put the box on the floor in front of me then reached back like I was going to hold on to the fireplace to get myself up, but instead I grabbed a handful of soot. I stood, with some effort, then kicked the box with my toe. It was heavy and only moved about six inches. Well, crap. I pushed it again with my foot. This time it moved three inches away.

By the third failed push, Grigsby lost his patience. He held the gun as he closed the distance between us, leaned over and grabbed the box.

The second he looked at his prize, I threw the soot in his face.

He bellowed as he raked the black ash from his eyes.

I scooped up the box and charged the door, but Grigsby recovered quickly. He lunged at me and tackled me to the floor. "I didn't want to hurt you, Nora. All you had to do was give me the box."

"Fine!" I screamed. "Take the box." I swung the metal case as hard as I could, and the corner of it connected with his head. Grigsby cried out as he rolled off me. His gun went off, and I felt a sharp sting in my leg.

I screamed again as he pounced on top of me. I hit him again. This time it connected with his jaw. Adrenaline charged through me, and I kept hitting Carl Grigsby until he stopped moving.

Only then did the energy drain from me, and I dropped the metal box.

"Nora!" I heard Ezra yelling.

"Help me," I whispered. Grigsby was still on top of me, and I didn't have the strength to move him away. "Please help."

"Call an ambulance," Ezra ordered. He was on the floor now, pushing the dirty cop over and away from me.

I stared at the too pale face of Grigsby. I couldn't tell if he was still breathing. "Is he dead?" I asked, my heart in my throat.

CHAPTER
TWENTY

"Please tell me he isn't dead." I'd wanted to hurt him, to get him to stop hurting *me*, but taking a life—that was something I never wanted to do.

McKay reached over and felt Grigsby's neck. "It's weak but he has a pulse." She looked at me, her eyes wide, confused, and scared. The shot must have sent them all into a panic. "What the hell happened?"

"It was him," I said. "Grigsby killed Lloyd." I started to cry as the adrenaline waned. "He shot me, Ezra."

"I've got you," he said. "It's not bad. You're going to be okay, Nora. I promise."

I hoped Ezra Holden took promises as seriously as I did. "The well house," I said. "What did you find?"

"The steamer trunk," he said. He smoothed back my hair and cupped my face. "You were right. He kept her body. He put her in the trunk with her purse. The driver's license indicates it's the skeletal remains of Maxine Garner."

"Good," I said. "Mr. Garner can put her to rest now."

Ezra gave me a weak smile. "*You* rest now." He kissed my forehead.

"Oh, and call Gilly and Pippa, okay? They'll want to know I'm going to the hospital."

"Yes." He chuckled. "I'll call them."

"Good."

"Will you let me take you out?" he asked.

"Right now?"

"I can wait until you've had some stitches."

"Ambulance is on the way," Reese said. "I called for two of them."

"Thanks," Ezra said. "Good work, Reese."

She gave me a tight smile. "Hang in there, Nora."

"I really don't feel that bad," I told Ezra.

"You don't?"

"My leg hurts, yes, but other than feeling worn the heck out, and a little sore, I'm okay."

"Do you want to get up?"

"Nope," I told him. "I kind of like having you hold me."

He grinned. "Me too."

"Ow," I told the doctor. "I don't think you got my leg very numb."

"It's a deep wound, Ms. Black. It's going to hurt," he said with more sarcasm than I liked.

Ezra had wanted to stay with me, but the doctor

kicked him out of the room. Stupid doctor. "Can you hurry?" I asked.

I could see Ezra's head peeking through the room's small window occasionally.

"Last suture," the doctor said. "There, done. I'll send a nurse in with your discharge orders."

"Okay, thanks."

Ezra came in as the doctor left and my mood lifted immensely.

"Everything okay?" he asked.

"Some damage to the muscle is all, no tendon or nerve. Doc says I'll make a full recovery."

He paced back and forth in front of the bed. "Good. Great. Great."

"Is something wrong?" I put my hand to my mouth. "Did Grigsby die?"

He stopped pacing. His shirt had been soiled with my blood, and he'd changed into hospital scrubs that were a little too small for his boxer build, and his muscles, especially in his arms, were like dinner and a show. Abruptly, he stared at me, his piercing green eyes raking over me with so much emotion it made my lungs squeeze. "No. He's still alive."

"Then what?" He'd been flirty banter-y Ezra on the ambulance ride over. Something had changed.

"You could have been killed, Nora."

"I know," I said. This was not news to me.

"It just hit me as I was standing out there in the hallway."

"I get it. Believe me. But I didn't die. Are you mad at me?"

He laughed softly. "No, I'm not mad at you."

"Then stop acting all weird and tell me what's on your mind?"

He sat down on the bed next to me, careful not to brush against my bad leg. The lines softened around his eyes as he reached out and brushed my hair away from my face. "*You're* on my mind," he said. He dipped his head and brushed his lips over mine, gently at first, but when I put my arms around his neck, he deepened the kiss until my entire body woke up, even the parts I feared were dead.

When the kiss finished, Ezra said, "Does this mean you'll let me take you out?"

"I'm not sure," I said, "I may need to sample the goods some more. I mean, as they say, why buy the cow when the milk is free."

"Am I the cow in this scenario?" He dipped down for another kiss, and this one made my toes curl.

"Wowza," I said, because I couldn't form real words.

"Is that a yes?"

I nodded. "Yep."

THREE WEEKS LATER...

"Didn't the doctor say to take it easy on that leg?" Gilly nagged. "You can aggravate the injury."

We stood outside a two-story Tudor-style home by

the lake. I used my cane to walk the cobblestone path to the front door.

"I'm not aggravating it," I said. "But you're aggravating *me*." This was worse than the poop-straining queries I'd dealt with for two months. "Besides, the stitches came out a week ago. I think I'm good."

All the charges had been dropped against Gilly, and Carl Grigsby was facing a lot of charges, but only if he woke up from his coma. I'd felt bad about nearly killing him, but not so bad that I wouldn't have done it again under the same circumstances. I'd learned my will to survive had outweighed bum knees, bad eyesight, and sheer exhaustion. Unfortunately, Phil Williams escaped any charges. I'd been the only one to hear Grigsby talk about him, and we all agreed that psychic scent visions did not count as actual evidence. However, Ezra is still investigating the douche bag, so that will have to be enough for now.

The skeletal remains had been definitively identified as Maxine Garner. Because of the circumstances, Mr. Garner was facing only months in prison, time served, instead of years for assault and obstruction. I'd agreed to take Godiva in until his hearing. She was great company, and I'd fallen hard for the little pocket beagle.

Oh, and while Ezra and I have not officially, gone out on a first date, unofficially, he has brought dinner over to my house every night since the shooting. I asked him to stop, because his excellent cooking was packing on the pounds. He suggested several seriously creative ways to burn off those extra calories. Let's just say, I have discovered *hard* evidence--pun intended--that sex after a hysterectomy is still pretty freaking spectacular. I swear, if he keeps it up, I might have to change my mind about buying the cow.

And now, I was doing something that I'd been thinking about all week, that I knew my mother would wholeheartedly approve of, but nonetheless, scared me witless.

Pippa carried the large box for me that I'd pulled out of storage. "I'm nervous," she said. "Do you think this is going to be okay? Maybe we should have waited."

"Don't be daft. It'll be fine." Now, I just needed to convince myself. As it were, I was quaking inside as I knocked on the front door.

A few seconds later, Leila Rafferty answered the door. She wore a pink and lemon-yellow scarf today, and the colors looked beautiful with her skin tone. "Hello," she said. "Can I help you?"

I was speechless for a moment as I thought of my mom. "Hi, I'm Nora. Nora Black. These are my friends, Gilly and Pippa."

The scent of lavender floated out into the air from behind Leila. My mother had used the essential oil for headaches and nausea during her treatments.

"She's just so aggravating," a man says. Once again, I recognize Shawn's voice. "I don't know why I got so mad at her." He sounds sad and weary. "I haven't talked to her other than to offer my sympathy in the past twenty years. Why did I let it get so heated?"

I know it's Leila in the room with him, because she is

wearing a lilac printed scarf on her head this time. She takes his hand. "You have to give yourself a break, Love. I'm sick, she's not. As brave as you're being for me, I know it's taking its toll. It's not hard to understand where your anger is coming from."

"I hope you know how much I love you," Shawn says.

"I know that, silly." She presses her palm against his heart. "I hope I meet her someday," she says.

"Why would you want to do that?"

"To thank her. Without Nora knowing it was time to move on, you wouldn't have found me. And for that gift, I will thank her a thousand times over."

Shawn snorts. "Don't get carried away." Leila giggles softly, and he embraces her in a tender hug. My heart breaks for them both.

That vision had to be from the night of the first time Shawn had summoned me to his office. I gulped back the knot in my throat as Leila frowned at me. I worried for a second that she was going to demand we leave, but then a slow smile formed on her lips.

"You're Shawn's Nora," she said. "Did you just do that thing," she touched the tip of her nose and wiggled it, "with your super sniffer? Shawn told me about it, and I can't tell you how much I've wanted to meet you. I have so many questions."

I chuckled nervously. "Well, I haven't been Shawn's Nora in a long time, but I've been wanting to meet you too." My lower lip began to quiver, but I managed to get it under control. "I don't want to take up a lot of your time," I said. "But I brought you…" Wow, now that I was here in front of Leila, I suddenly felt like a presumptuous busybody. "I hope you don't mind, and if you want me to take them back, I'll understand."

"What is it?" Leila asked.

"My mother. Uhm. I don't know if Shawn told you about her. She died last year."

She nodded. "He did. I'm so sorry for your loss."

"Thank you." I urged Pippa forward and opened the top of the box. "These are my mother's wigs. All top of the line, real hair, and lace fronts. I've been holding onto them..." I tried to dam the tears, but they would not be stopped. "I don't know if you're even interested in wearing wigs, but I think it would've made my mom very happy for you to have them."

Leila wiped a tear from her eye, and I heard Gilly and Pippa sniffle. What a bunch we were. Finally, Leila nodded. "I'll take them on one condition."

"What?"

"That you all come in and have some iced tea with me. It's a beautiful day, and I could use the company."

I smiled at her. "We'd love to."

The End...

Read For Whom the Smell Tolls (A Nora Black Midlife Psychic Mystery Book 2) Next!

My name is Nora Black. I'm over fifty and enjoying my life to the fullest. That is, when I'm not worried about graying hair, low back pain, sagging skin, and a psychic gift that sometimes stinks.

After solving a murder with the help of my new scent-induced psychic ability, I'm thrilled to report that everything is finally getting back to normal. Better than normal, actually. My BFFs work with me at my Scents & Scentsability shop, I'm dating a young, hot detective, and the upcoming Memorial Day Weekend promises to bring in lots of happy-to-spend-money tourists to Garden Cove.

There's not a thing in this world that could spoil my great mood...

Nothing except a suspicious death. When police officer Reese McKay asks me to use my aroma-mojo to look into the "accidental drowning" of her black-sheep cousin, I can't turn her away. Especially now she's become a friend. There are only two problems--allergies have clogged my sinuses and have affected my ability to smell, and my ex, the chief of police, is less than thrilled that I'm sticking my nose into another investigation.

With help from my besties Gilly and Pippa, along with an unofficial assist from Detective Hot Stuff, I'm determined to crack the case of the drowned girl and sniff out the killer before he or she can strike again.

WANT MORE COZY MYSTERY SERIES?
Check Out Barkside of the Moon Mysteries!
Pit Perfect Murder (Barkside of the Moon Cozy Mysteries Book 1)

When cougar-shifter Lily Mason moves to Moonrise, Missouri, she wishes for only three things from the town and its human population. . . to find a job, to find a place to live, and to live as a human, not a therianthrope.

Lily gets more than she bargains for when a rescue pit bull named Smooshie rescues her from an oncoming car, and it's love at first sight. Thanks to Smooshie, Lily's first two wishes are granted by Parker Knowles, the owner of the Pit Bull Rescue center, who offers her a job at the shelter and the room over his garage for rent.

Lily's new life as an integrator is threatened when Smooshie finds Katherine Kapersky, the local church choir leader and head of the town council, dead in the field behind the rescue center. Unfortunately, there are more suspects than mourners for the elderly town leader. Can Lily keep her less-than-human status under wraps? Or will the killer, who has pulled off a nearly Pit Perfect murder, expose her to keep Lily and her dog from digging up the truth?

FOR WHOM THE SMELL TOLLS

A NORA BLACK MIDLIFE PSYCHIC MYSTERY
BOOK TWO

Chapter One

"I've made a decision, Nora. You're not going to like it, but I really need you to be okay with it." Gilly Martin, my best friend in the world, hit me with her most earnest gaze. "I hope I'll have your support."

It was five o'clock in the afternoon, and we were finishing the closing cleanup of Scents & Scentsability, my spa boutique in Garden Cove. Since I'd added the massage component, Gilly's part of the business, the sales of our lotions, massage oils, and soaps had doubled.

I shook my head. "Please don't tell me you're pregnant," I said teasingly as I wiped the inside of the front door, but the darkening in Gilly's brown eyes made me gasp. "You're pregnant? How? Why?" I asked, appalled at the idea. "For the love of Pete, you're fifty-one years old, Gillian Judith Martin. You have two teenagers getting ready to start their senior year. Why would you want to start over?"

Gilly's frown deepened for a second, then her lip began to tremble. Was she going to cry?

"I'm sorry!" I said quickly. "Of course, I support you. I'm here for you no matter what."

A choking sound bubbled from her lips as she turned away from me.

"Please don't cry." I was a terrible BFF. Gilly needed my understanding, my patience, my love—not my judgement. "I'll even take those awful Bradley childbirth breathing classes with you if you want."

Now she was in a full-on sob...or at least, I thought.

"Are you laughing?"

"Nora, you are so gullible." She slapped the counter and wheezed. "I can't catch my breath."

Her laughter verged on hysteria. I was not amused. "You're a butthead," I informed her with a raised brow.

"I never said I was pregnant," Gilly answered. "But your assumption is hilarious. You should have seen your face." Her whole body shook with laughter and she literally slapped her knee. "Priceless."

I rolled my eyes. "Fine, fine." I put down the Windex bottle. "Why do you need my support?"

She straightened, suddenly sobered, and with calm measure, she declared, "I've decided to grow out the gray in my hair."

Nooooooo! This was far worse than a *whoops baby* in my book. I took a few slow, deep breaths, then summoned my strength. "That's so amazingly great." I stared at her chestnut-brown hair. It was pulled back into a braid, which was the way she liked to wear it when she worked. I could see the rich brown of her hairline, which meant she'd colored it recently. "I'm here for you. Totally," I added.

"It's a good thing you don't make a living as a spy, because you're saying one thing, but your face," she circled her finger at me, "is telling me a whole 'nother story."

The idea of watching Gilly grow gray was like watching my own mortality. I wasn't sure I was ready for it. "When did you decide this?"

"Been thinking about it for a while now. The gray is growing out faster than every six weeks. I have to do touch-ups at home every couple of weeks now in between trips to the salon."

"I do my own color. It's not that big of a deal. I can teach you."

She placed her hands on her rounded hips. "I'm going gray, Nora, and that's the end of this conversation."

I winced. "It's your life."

It was Gilly's turn to roll her eyes. "It's my hair, not my life."

I raised my brows but left it at that. "Can you believe Pippa is learning how to drive a motorcycle?" I asked, changing the subject.

"She's going to break her flippin' neck!" Gilly exclaimed. Gilly had been ranting about Pippa's decision for a week now, so I knew the redirection would work.

207

"Just because her biker barista rides, doesn't mean she has to do it. I mean, she's younger than us, but she's still no spring chicken."

I looked around as if our thirty-something friend might overhear Gilly's complaints even though I knew Pippa was spending time with her guy on this lovely Wednesday afternoon. This was her only chance for time off, considering we were two days away from Memorial Day weekend, one of the biggest tourism weekends of the year.

"Pippa will be fine," I reassured Gilly, even though I wasn't exactly convinced myself.

"I wish you had futuristic visions, instead of seeing past memories. I'd feel a lot safer knowing that Pippa would be safe on that crotch rocket."

"There are no guarantees in life," I said. "And the only way to stop Pippa from riding a motorcycle is to hog-tie her then lock her in your basement until the end of time."

"Works for me," muttered Gilly. "When's the last time you smelled her?"

Oh for the love of Pete's pits. I'd had enough of being forced to sniff my friends. After dying for twenty-seven seconds during my hysterectomy, I'd woken up with a nose that could literally smell trouble. At least if that trouble was contained in the memories of other people. It seemed to work as long as the odor evoked strong emotions, so the visions weren't all bad, thank heavens.

The first several weeks after finding out about my new smell-o-vision gift, Gilly and Pippa had constantly made me smell them—like, all day, every day—to test my ability. As a result, I now knew way more about my two closest gal pals than I wanted to or should. I was so happy when the shiny newness of my ability finally wore off, and they stopped shoving their wrists under my nose.

"Jordy will make sure she's safe," I said.

I'd given Jordy Hines, the tattooed owner of Moo-La-Lattes and Pippa's new beau, a lecture about Pippa wearing a helmet and pads at all times that served as a not-so thinly veiled threat. Pippa was like our younger sister. And we followed the sibling rule: We were allowed to torture her, but we'd junk-punch anyone else who hurt her.

"Are we still on for dinner tonight?" Gilly asked.

"Of course, we are."

My BFF had been a little lost this past week, because her ex-husband, Giovanni Rossi, had called a few weeks back and asked if the teen twins could fly out to Vegas to spend time with him. She'd never spent more than a night or two away from her dynamic duo, and their absence was taking its toll. Next summer, the twins would graduate high school and go off to college. I couldn't imagine what Gilly would be like without her children around for months at a time. It would probably feel like getting fired from motherhood.

I'd made a standing date with her for every day the kids were gone, and since they still had one more day in Vegas, I was Gilly's for the night. She needed the company, and in all fairness, she'd done as much or more for me, especially when I'd dealt with the last harrowing months of my mother's terminal cancer. Gilly had been a rock for me, offering a safe space to break down when I felt overwhelmed.

Gilly walked past me and gave me a hip bump. "I feel bad keeping you from Detective Hottie."

"Ezra's been busy with work and such," I said. The "and such" was actually Ezra's teenaged son, Mason. The sixteen-year-old boy was staying with him while Ezra's ex-wife, Kati Portman, and her resort-owner husband went on a two-week vacation to the Bahamas. Ezra hadn't introduced me to his son yet, but also, I hadn't asked for an introduction.

I'd never had kids. Being the godmother of Gilly's teens was the closest I'd ever gotten to motherhood. And I was happy with my choice not to have had children. Still, a part of me would have liked Ezra to, at least, *want* me to meet his kid. I mean, while we hadn't exactly defined our relationship, we were more than just mattress buddies.

"Is there trouble in paradise?" Gilly teased. When I didn't answer right away, Gilly narrowed her gaze. "You know I'm not serious, right? Are things okay between you and Easy?" Easy was Ezra's nickname, used by co-workers and friends. I called him Ezra, but I wasn't above teasing Mr. Easy Like Sunday Morning.

"Ezra and I are awesome," I said, not wanting to delve too deeply into what might or might not be going on between Ezra and me. "Like I said, he's been busy, is all. You know how it is with kids around."

"Oh, that's right. He has his son. For how much longer?"

"Until next weekend."

"I still can't believe Big Don let Roger go away over Memorial weekend."

Donald Portman owned Portman's on the Lake, one of the big five resorts in Garden Cove. His son Roger managed the place for him, and eight years ago, Roger married Ezra's ex-wife, Kati. Ezra had relocated to the area to be closer to Mason. I hadn't been around then; my career had taken me to Chicago. But I'd grown up with Roger. He was a year older than Gilly and me, and he'd always been a showboat.

"I can't believe Big Don let Roger go on vacation at all, much less during the busiest tourist weekend of the year." I shrugged. "Maybe the old coot was feeling generous."

"Hah!" Gilly clucked her tongue. "Big Don doesn't have a generous bone in his body. And believe me, I know. The man wagged his ungenerous bone at me once when he'd stopped in for a massage at the Rose Palace."

I swallowed back a gag. "That's disgusting."

"I wish he was the worst person I'd ever run into at the Rose Palace."

Until recently, Gilly had been the spa manager at the Rose Palace Resort. That is, until Phil Williams, the jackhole who ran the resort, had fired her after she'd gotten arrested for a murder she didn't commit. Phil had been up to his filthy eyeballs in the death of Gilly's ex-boyfriend, Lloyd Briscoll. Unfortunately, the only person who could connect Phil to Lloyd's murder was the actual killer, Carl Grigsby, a dirty cop on Phil's payroll. He told me about Phil right before shooting me. The bullet had ripped through my leg, and I hadn't given him another chance to aim better.

I beat him into a coma. My ex-husband, Shawn who happened to be the chief of police, had ordered police protection around the clock for the time being, just in case Phil got it in his head to take out the only witness to his connection to Lloyd.

Sometimes, I went to the hospital to sit with him. I'm not sure why. I didn't feel guilty for knocking his head in. It was him or me. Carl Grigsby had totally deserved it. But it wasn't justice. He needed to wake up so he could face the consequences of his actions, for the arsons, the murder, and for shooting me.

"I'm glad you're working here now," I told her. "With me." I put my arm around her shoulder. "And you no longer have to deal with lecherous men looking for happy endings."

Gilly laughed. "That's the God's truth." She put away the last of the cleaning supplies in the utility closet. "Let's get out of here."

After turning off the lights, turning on the alarm, and locking the door, we separated on the sidewalk. Since early-bird tourists were already in Garden Cove, parking spaces were scarce. Gilly had parked two blocks down in a public lot on the other side of Dolly's Dollhouse Emporium, but I'd gotten to work early enough to get a space one block over near the courthouse.

I smiled when I saw a familiar face coming up the sidewalk. "Reese, how nice to see you." Reese McKay, a young patrol officer, had been one of the cops on the scene the night I'd been shot. As a matter of fact, she'd been Carl Grigsby's unlucky partner. No one had been more shocked about Carl's seedy side than her.

She smiled back and waved. "Hey, Nora. Nice day, huh?" She looked up at the clear blue sky and shielded her eyes from the sun before pivoting her gaze back to me. "I hope this keeps up for the weekend."

"Same," I replied. I dug my keys from my purse. "It's going to be a busy weekend."

"Tell me about it." She sighed. "I don't know who's worse, the drunk and rowdy tourists stirring up trouble or the small-time crooks in Garden Cove trying to rip them off. It's a nightmare."

She wore a pair of jeans and a butter-yellow tank top. Her strawberry-blonde hair was down around her shoulders, and the wind kept whipping strands about her face.

I jangled my keys. "I don't want to keep you from your errands."

Reese snorted as she pushed the offending hair away, and she looked back toward the courthouse. "I wish you were interrupting errands."

"Is something wrong?"

"Always," she said. "At least where my cousin Fiona is concerned. She had a court appearance this afternoon."

Since Reese had instigated the information, so I

didn't feel too much like a nosy Parker when I asked, "Anything serious?"

"Damn girl ran a red light then blew a point-one-five on the breathalyzer. It's her second DUI in less than a year. And the last one was only two and half months ago."

"That's not good."

"Tell me about it."

"Where's she at now? Did they lock her up or something?" A blood alcohol over point-one-five carried a minimum jail time, along with fines and license suspension. I only knew this because my dad, God rest his soul, used to be Garden Cove's police chief. Now, my ex-husband, Shawn Rafferty, was the guy in charge.

"Nothing like that, though she'd probably be better off facing some real consequences. The prosecutor is an old friend of my uncle Reagan. Reagan owns half the commercial real estate here in town, so the prosecutor cut Fiona a break. She's paying the fine right now, and her license has been suspended for a year, plus she has to attend AA meetings."

"Sounds like she could use the meetings."

"You don't get sober just because a judge orders it." I detected the bitter tone of experience in her words. "I'll believe it when I see it."

"Well, hopefully this is a wake-up call for her."

A young woman with thick auburn hair and a body that rivaled J-Lo's, including the curvy booty, trotted up behind Reese. "Hey, Cuz," she said. "Ready to go?"

Reese rolled her eyes. "Yep." She nodded toward me. "Nora Black, this is my cousin, Fiona McKay."

Her eyes widened with delight. "Nora Black of Scents and Scentsability?"

"One and the same," I replied.

Fiona scooted around Reese, threw open her arms and hugged me. She had a wide, gold-toned cuff bracelet on her left wrist, and it dug into my back.

"It's so nice to meet you," she gushed. "I love your lotions." She held her bangle-free wrist up to my face. "I'm wearing your blond sandalwood and rosemary lotion right now. God, it's yummy."

It *was* yummy.

It also triggered a vision.

"Come on, sugar," Fiona said. Like all my scent-induced visions, I couldn't see her face, but her voice, her hair, and her body made it quite evident this was her memory. "You promised to give me a taste."

A tall, thin man wearing a western shirt, a bolo tie, jeans that bagged a little, and pointy-toed, red and black cowboy boots, leaned his fuzzed-out face into hers. I heard some disgusting smacking of lips and tongues.

After they finished kissing, the guy said, "I can't deny you anything, dumpling." He reached into his pocket and pulled out a small vial of white powder. "I got your candy right here."

He opened the top and dabbed the drugs onto the meaty part of Fiona's hand. I caught a glimpse of a watch with a dark face and some gold lines.

"Are you all right?" Fiona asked, alarmed. "Hello?

Reese's Pieces, I think there's something wrong with your friend."

Reese stared at me expectantly. "Did you just...?"

I nodded. She was aware of my scratch-n-sniff psychic ability to tap into other people's memories. I tried to convey my horror at what I'd seen, but Reese shook her head. "Forget it. I don't want to know."

"What?" asked Fiona, frowning as she looked from me to her cousin. "What are you guys talking about?"

"Nothing," said Reese. "See you later, Nora." She grabbed her cousin by the arm and hauled her down the sidewalk and away from me.

Reese hadn't wanted to know about the memory. Was it because she suspected her cousin was into more than booze? My heart broke a little for the both of them.

Want more? Click Here!

PIT PERFECT MURDER
BARKSIDE OF THE MOON COZY MYSTERIES
BOOK 1

Chapter 1 - Sneak Peek

When I was eighteen years old, I came home from a sleepover and found my mom and dad with their throats cut, and their hearts ripped from their chests.

My little brother Danny was in a broom closet in the kitchen, his arms wrapped around his knees, and his face pale and ghostly. Until that day, I'd planned to go to college and study medicine after graduation, but instead, I ended up staying home and taking care of my seven-year-old brother.

Seventeen years later, my brother was murdered. At the time, Danny's death looked like it would go unsolved, much like my parents' had.

Without Haze Kinsey, my best friend since we were five, the killers would have gotten away with it. She was a special agent for the FBI for almost a decade, and when I called her about Danny's death, she dropped everything to come help me get him justice. The evil group of witches and Shifters responsible for the decimation of my family paid with their lives.

Yes. I said witches and Shifters. Did I forget to mention I'm a werecougar? Oh, and my friend Hazel is a witch. Recently, I discovered witches in my own family tree on my mother's side. Shifters, in general, only mated with Shifters, but witches were the exception. As a matter of fact, my friend Haze is mated to a bear Shifter.

I wouldn't have known about the witch in my genealogy, though, if a rogue witch coven hadn't done some funky hoodoo witchery to me. Apparently, the spell activated a latent talent that had been dormant in my hybrid genes.

My ancestor's magic acted like truth serum to anyone who came near her. No one could lie in her presence. Lucky me, my ability was a much lesser form of hers. People didn't have to tell me the truth, but whenever they were around me, they had the compulsion to overshare all sorts of private matters about themselves. This can get seriously uncomfortable for all parties involved. Like, the fact that I didn't need to know that Janet Strickland had been wearing the same pair of underwear for an entire week, or that Mike Dandridge had sexual fantasies about clowns.

My newfound talent made me unpopular and unwelcome in a town full of paranormal creatures who thrived on little deceptions. So, when Haze discovered the whereabouts of my dad's brother, a guy I hadn't known even existed, I sold all my belongings, let the bank have my parents' house, jumped in my truck, and headed south.

After two days and 700 miles of nonstop gray, snowy weather, I pulled my screeching green and yellow mini-truck into an auto repair shop called The Rusty Wrench. Much like my beloved pickup, I'd needed a new start, and moving to a small town occupied by humans seemed the best shot. I'd barely made it to Moonrise, Missouri before my truck began its death throes. The vehicle protested the last 127 miles by sputtering to a halt as I rolled her into the closest spot.

The shop was a small white-brick building with a one-car garage off to the right side. A black SUV and a white compact car occupied two of the six parking spots.

A sign on the office door said: *No Credit Cards. Cash Only. Some Local Checks Accepted (Except from Earl—You Know Why, Earl! You check-bouncing bastard).*

A man in stained coveralls, wiping a greasy tool with a rag, came out the side door of the garage. He had a full head of wavy gray hair, bushy eyebrows over light blue, almost colorless eyes, and a minimally lined face that made me wonder about his age. I got out of the truck to greet him.

"Can I help you, miss?" His voice was soft and raspy with a strong accent that was not quite Deep South.

"Yes, please." I adjusted my puffy winter coat. "The heater stopped working first. Then the truck started jerking for the last fifty miles or so."

He scratched his stubbly chin. "You could have

thrown a rod, sheared the distributor, or you have a bad ignition module. That's pretty common on these trucks."

I blinked at him. I could name every muscle in the human body and twelve different kinds of viruses, but I didn't know a spark plug from a radiator cap. "And that all means..."

"If you threw a rod, the engine is toast. You'll need a new vehicle."

"Crap." I grimaced. "What if it's the other thingies?"

The scruffy mechanic shrugged. "A sheared distributor is an easy fix, but I have to order in the part, which means it won't get fixed for a couple of days. Best-case scenario, it's the ignition module. I have a few on hand. Could get you going in a couple of hours, but..." he looked over my shoulder at the truck and shook his head, "...I wouldn't get your hopes up."

I must've looked really forlorn because the guy said, "It might not need any parts. Let me take a look at it first. You can grab a cup of coffee across the street at Langdon's One-Stop."

He pointed to the gas station across the road. It didn't look like much. The pale-blue paint on the front of the building looked in need of a new coat, and the weather-beaten sign with the store's name on it had seen better days. There was a car at the gas pumps and a couple more in the parking lot, but not enough to call it busy.

I'd had enough of one-stops, though, thank you. The bathrooms had been horrible enough to make a wereraccoon yark, and it took a lot to make those garbage eaters sick. Besides, I wasn't just passing through Moonrise, Missouri.

"Have you ever heard of The Cat's Meow Café?" Saying the name out loud made me smile the way it had when Hazel had first said it to me. I'd followed my GPS into town, so I knew I wasn't too far away from the place.

"Just up the street about two blocks, take a right on Sterling Street. You can't miss it. I should have some news in about an hour or so, but take your time."

"Thank you, Mister..."

"Greer." He shoved the tool in his pocket. "Greer Knowles."

"I'm Lily Mason."

"Nice to meet ya," said Greer. "The place gets hoppin' around noon. That's when church lets out."

I looked at my phone. It was a little before noon now. "Good. I could go for something to eat. How are the burgers?"

"Best in town," he quipped.

I laughed. "Good enough."

Even in the sub-freezing temperature, my hands were sweating in my mittens. I wasn't sure what had me more nervous, leaving the town I grew up in for the first time in my life or meeting an uncle I'd never known existed.

I crossed a four-way intersection. One of the signs was missing, and I saw the four-by-four post had snapped off at its base. I hadn't noticed it on my way in. Crap. Had I run a stop sign? I walked the two blocks to

Sterling. The diner was just where Greer had said. A blue truck, a green mini-coup, and a sheriff's SUV were parked out front.

An alarm dinged as the glass door opened to The Cat's Meow. Inside, there was a row of six booths along the wall, four tables that seated four out in the open floor, and counter seating with about eight cushioned black stools. The interior décor was rustic country with orange tabby kitsch everywhere. A man in blue jeans and a button-down shirt with a string tie sat in the nearest booth. A female police officer sat at a counter chair sipping coffee and eating a cinnamon roll. Two elderly women, one with snowball-white hair, the other a dyed strawberry-blonde, sat in a back booth.

The white poof-headed lady said, "This egg is not over-medium."

"Well, call the mayor," said Redhead. "You're unhappy with your eggs. Again."

"See this?" She pointed at the offending egg. "Slime, right here. Egg snot. You want to eat it?"

"If it'll make you shut up about breakfast food, I'll eat it and lick the plate."

A man with copper-colored hair and a thick beard, tall and well-muscled, stepped out of the kitchen. He wore a white apron around his waist, and he had on a black T-shirt and blue jeans. He held a plate with a single fried egg shining in the middle.

The old woman with the snowy hair blushed, her thin skin pinking up as he crossed the room to their table. "Here you go, Opal. Sorry 'bout the mix-up on your egg." He slid the plate in front of her. "This one is pure perfection." He grinned, his broad smile shining. "Just like you." He winked.

Opal giggled.

The redhead rolled her eyes. "You're as easy as the eggs."

"Oh, Pearl. You're just mad he didn't flirt with you."

As the women bickered over the definition of flirting, the cook glanced at me. He seemed startled to see me there. "You can sit anywhere," he said. "Just pick an open spot."

"I'm actually looking for someone," I told him.

"Who?"

"Daniel Mason." Saying his name gave me a hollow ache. My parents had named my brother Daniel, which told me my dad had loved his brother, even if he didn't speak about him.

The man's brows rose. "And why are you looking for him?"

I immediately knew he was a werecougar like me. The scent was the first clue, and his eyes glowing, just for a second, was another. "You're Daniel Mason, aren't you?"

He moved in closer to me and whispered barely audibly, but with my Shifter senses, I heard him loud and clear. "I go by Buzz these days."

"Who's your new friend, Buzz?" the policewoman asked. Now that she was looking up from her newspaper, I could see she was young.

He flashed a charming smile her way. "Never you

mind, Nadine." He gestured to a waitress, a middle-aged woman with sandy-colored hair, wearing a black T-shirt and a blue jean skirt. "Top off her coffee, Freda. Get Nadine's mind on something other than me."

"That'll be a tough 'un, Buzz." Freda laughed. "I don't think Deputy Booth comes here for the cooking."

"More like the cook," the elderly lady with the light strawberry-blonde hair said. She and her friend cackled.

The policewoman's cheeks turned a shade of crimson that flattered her chestnut-brown hair and pale complexion. "Y'all mind your P's and Q's."

Buzz chuckled and shook his head. He turned his attention back to me. "Why is a pretty young thing like you interested in plain ol' me?"

I detected a slight apprehension in his voice.

"If you're Buzz Mason, I'm Lily Mason, and you're my uncle."

The man narrowed his dark-emerald gaze at me. "I think we'd better talk in private."

Keep Reading!

About the Author

I am a USA Today Bestselling author who writes paranormal mysteries and romances because I love all things whodunit, Otherworldly, and weird. Also, I wish my pittie, the adorable Kona Princess Warrior and my two cats Ash and Simon could talk. Or at least be more like Scooby-Doo and help me unmask villains at the haunted house up the street.

When I'm not writing about mystery-solving were-cougars or the adventures of a hapless psychic living among shapeshifters, I am preyed upon by stray kittens who end up living in my house because I can't say no to those sweet, furry faces. (Someone stop telling them where I live!)

I live in Mid-Missouri with my family and I spend my non-writing time doing really cool stuff...like watching TV and cleaning up dog poop

Follow Renee!
Bookbub
Renee's Rebel Readers FB Group
Newsletter

Printed in Great Britain
by Amazon